The Secret of Hurricanes

A Novel by

Theresa Williams

MacAdam/Cage Publishing
155 Sansome Street, Suite 550
San Francisco, CA 94104
www.macadamcage.com

Library of Congress Cataloging-in-Publication Data

Williams, Theresa, 1956 —
    The secret of hurricanes / by Theresa Williams.
        p. cm.
    ISBN 1-931561-10-9 (alk. paper)
      1. Women weavers–Fiction.
2. Middle aged women–Fiction. 3. Pregnant women–
Fiction. 4. Hurricanes–Fiction. I. Title.

    PS3623.I565 S43 2002
    813'.6–dc21

                                                    2002006484

Manufactured in the United States of America.
10 9 8 7 6 5 4 3 2 1

Book design by Dorothy Carico Smith.
Jacket design by Frances Baca.

Grateful acknowledgment is made to South-Western College
Publishing for permission to publish an excerpt from *Century 21
Typewriting Advanced* © 1977. Reprinted with permission of
South-Western College Publishing, a division of Thomson
Learning.

The Secret of Hurricanes

A Novel by

Theresa Williams

MacAdam/Cage

for Allen

…My story
gets told in various ways: a romance,
a dirty joke, a war, a vacancy.

—*Rumi*

PART I

ONE

That article in the Waterville *Scout* said it was Shakespearean, all that fatalism that guides the Kennedys' lives. The likelihood of untimely death. Recently, another one died in his prime, John-John in an airplane. Not long before that, Bobby's boy. While playing football at high speeds on snow skis.

Those Kennedys take some crazy chances.

I prefer my own easy ways.

Which isn't to say my life hasn't been Shakespearean.

By the time I was sixteen, my life was like the darkened stage at the end of *Hamlet* or *Macbeth*. All littered with corpses and treachery.

Unlike some Kennedys, I survived.

The *Scout* said those Kennedys are always showing family movies. Saying, "There's Bobby" and "There's Jack." Their dead are always with them, the

Scout said.

As are mine.

I hear the dead oftentimes: parents, friends, lovers. Some gnawing at the undersides of grasses. Wanting to be coaxed out with sweet words like *It's all right. I love you.*

Others wanting to know how they're being remembered: *Do you think this is how I planned my life?*

Some set foot in my home. Inspect the backs of cabinets. Refrigerator's cold remains. Vents and pipes for what's been cast off: *How much of this is what you mean to leave behind?*

In my bed, they sometimes lie between the sheets. Some stare into the dark like grumpy lovers. Some want things they never had. Mourning every ambushed glittering thing.

There's no homesickness like this.

TWO

People can't stand the secrecy of others.

They all want to know who the father is. Who your father is. Who was crazy enough to lie with Pearl Starling, now forty-five, woman with such a colorful past.

These days when I walk into the IGA, belly pushed out before me in this new millennium like a badge I'm proud to wear, most people's faces twist in amusement. Disgust. And a curiosity they try to hide.

Not exactly the kind of woman to make a man burn with passion. Always been plain, too plain to describe, they think, *and now a hermit besides. Unplucked brows, lopsided collars, earth beneath the nails. Strange face.*

Yes, strange, having forgotten the art of the strained smile.

Not only that, I wear odd hats.

Yesterday, a woman came up to me at the IGA. It was Moreen, a classmate from high school. My canvas hat, olive drab and beatup about the brim, cut off my view of everything but her feet, clad in hard plastic shoes. High heels.

"Just wondering," Moreen said.

She wasn't standing too close. Yet I caught her scent. The eye-burning sting of new clothes, still stiff with commodity starch. "Why don't you go someplace else? Huh?" she asked. Wobbling on tiny spikes. "Think about your baby!"

Oh, how she made my stomach cramp.

When I was small, and my family used to eat supper together, Daddy made me eat everything on my plate. To that last bit of gristle. Mama would wrap the bitter thing in a piece of sweet biscuit so I could get it down.

With Moreen, no difference. *Think about your baby!* Gristled heart wrapped in sweet concern. And I was supposed to swallow this. Vexation upon vexation. It never ends.

Also, yesterday, after the grocery. Who should come to my home? The Pentecostals from Waterville Holiness just down the road. You see what I mean? Two women, one old and one young. Sisters in the Lord. From the kitchen window, I studied them. How they walked. How they stepped off the asphalt into the weeds for cars to pass. How the young one worried about her little white socks. About those sticky seeds that hitch rides on the ankles of travelers. How she bent and tried to brush them off. The old one, oblivious to such earthly concerns. Those Pentecostals!

Every day they gather in that white box to scream at God. To speak in that language only He understands. You can hear them from the road. "Ai! Ai! Ai!" Also the moaning. Grave murmurings.

Once, I do admit, I succumbed. After all, they're experts. Specialists in seismology, eruptions and upheaval, faults and quakes. Delicate movements within. The smallest shifting of the human heart.

When I was fifteen and death was all around me, I went to their altar, prayed. Returned the next night and the next. The next, the next, the next. A drunkard, a sponge, intoxicated by the laying on of hands. By men holding my head in their hands, praying. Their eyes closed as if darkness gave them this sanction to touch. Crying sometimes in their dark. Like lovers.

In time I came to hate it, that kind of touching. It felt more like an invasion than love.

No, they've never forgotten I once was one of them. That I boarded their ancient creaking bus, lurched my way to coastal towns spreading the word of God. And so they still come knocking at my door every now and then.

Yesterday, the old one and the young one stood at my gate. Two women I'd never seen before. And the old one unlatched the door like a servant and let the young one walk through.

I've forgotten what it's like to have gates opened for me, Daughter. And doors. To have hands offer themselves to me in that gentle way just because I exist. That was Zeke's way.

Once, two weeks after Lydia Hunnycutt had died, Zeke Bell and I were in the graveyard, our backs against her cold stone. I told Zeke, "I'm old. Already old." His hand flattened against my chest. Pressed hard as though to stop bleeding.

This touch and my body opened. It opened like a gate. It opened like a hand. Like a warm hand, the clean hand of possibility.

All this I was thinking. As the Pentecostals marched up to my trailer door.

The old one knocked. Boldly. Confidently. Knowing God was on her side. Her heavy drumming had the weight of ceremony.

"What!" I yelled.

The young one turned her head, strained to see me. But the window screen, I knew, was nothing but a dark rectangle in the Carolina sun. She squinted. Imagined she saw an elbow. Part of a face. I'm sure her heart surged thinking about me, the strange woman on the other side.

I'm sure she was thinking, *It's like talking to the dead.*

Thinking, *There's all kinds of things I want to know.*

I know what it's like being young. I know the young one wanted to know what it's like being with men. And whether or not they all make love the same. She's imagined how it is. Something like bodies unfolding in the presence of each other. Like moss roses unfolding to the sun.

I'm sure she wanted to know, too, what it's like to be with a boy whose heart's in the grave next to his lover.

And what it's like to see a man's head explode, his dreams spatter your clothes.

But mostly, like everybody else, I'm certain she wanted to know who your father is.

The old Pentecostal looked steadfastly at the door, wanting to know too. Behind her the open sky. Deceitful sky.

Back straight, ankles together, the old one frowned. God's Nazi. "Hello," she said. Unfriendly. Such authority! She wasn't one for asking but for telling. It was, very clearly, an order for me to open the door.

They both faced the door. Shoulders squared. Soldiers.

I knew from past dealings, they had come to promise me eternity. If only I'd open the damn door.

THREE

My first memory is of the Grand Canyon.

I was two years old. We were moving from Twentynine Palms, California, to Waterville, North Carolina. Daddy'd retired from the Marine Corps and wanted to live in a town like Waterville that was close to Camp LaGrange, where he could take advantage of his base privileges. A town that had cheap land. He was out for a new start, he'd told Mama. Mama said he'd told her moving to Waterville would be like being a pioneer, except they'd be going in the opposite direction, West to East. From desert and big sky to salty air and hurricanes. The Grand Canyon was just a little stop along the way, a place to stretch our legs, a place to take in sights.

I saw some sights. Daddy held me upside down by one ankle over a barrier. Dangling over that wide gap in the Earth, my ankle twisting in Daddy's hand,

I found it startling, all that space. Sky below me, sky above. Birds circling—crosses against the sky. Mama saying, "Wade, please. Please don't. Please, Wade. Don't." Over and over. Quietly. Ever so quietly so nobody would hear.

Daddy laughing, saying, "It's only a little fun."

When I was twelve or so, I mentioned it to Mama.

A waste.

"It *never happened!*" she said. "Birds! No birds can live that high." That was proof, she said. Proof it was a dream. Besides, I was only two. And people can't remember that far back, so she claimed.

But it wasn't a dream. And I do remember.

The birds, the sky.

So much sky.

When I cried out, birds scattered to distant cliffs. Traitors hunched on some safe rock. Watched. Waited for my slow fall.

Ever since, big spaces have troubled me.

And most birds.

FOUR

Waterville is a place of holy war. Here, even in this new millennium, churches and bars rival for men's souls.

From the first night we arrived in Waterville, Daddy preferred the bars. Yes, I was only two, but I remember how he left Mama and me alone for two nights. In a motel called The Dixie, a room with split linoleum and rusted walls. Mama talked to me about that place sometimes, commenting on the roaches, the filth. How the first thing she'd seen when she unlocked the door and gone in was the mussed bed, bloody spots on the sheets. I don't remember the bed myself, but Mama's descriptions were always memorable. Mama was a clean woman. Very clean. Squalor and dirt—the two main things in life she couldn't stand.

Mama and I stayed at The Dixie while Daddy

roved. It was on our third night in Waterville that he brought us here, to our new home. A silver night, moon eerily lighting fog. Daddy, reeking of smoke and sweat and beer, brought us to this place, to this trailer on three acres. Where I live still. Right here, in the same trailer, on this piece of ground on Hunnycutt Road.

During all the years Daddy lived in Waterville, he spent most of his time at General Patton's—later called Saigon Sal's—telling the barmaids his family didn't understand him. He might have come to Waterville to start a new life, Mama once told me, but when we got here it was the same old thing. Same sorry life as when he was stationed at Twentynine Palms. And when he was stationed at Parris Island before that. In Waterville he came home several nights a week with his face greasy from other women's lips, the smell of sweaty barstools on his clothes.

Most of the places like Saigon Sal's are gone now. Replaced by Tiki Clubs and Thunderbird Inns. Franchises. Buildings with glass doors, neon signs. Upscale. Oh yes, this town has grown. Indoor mall. Wal-Mart. Home Depot. Red Lobster. Outback. Wild economic growth, unplanned, unchecked, like a cancer. More apartments and houses than you could believe.

I read all the time in the *Scout* about towns losing themselves to urban sprawl. But Waterville was always lost. Always soulless, despite the churches. Waterville wasn't a good place for us to live. It fed Daddy's vices, every one. Women. Beer. Desire for fame, however fleeting, however small.

- - -

When I was three or four, I remember Mama coming out of the bedroom she and Daddy shared, wearing a yellowed slip with torn lace and busted seams. Daddy was still in bed. And Mama stood over the kitchen sink like someone gone crazy and laughed wildly, laughed into the open drain. Her face all snot and tears. "Your family don't understand you? You tell that to all your whores? That's goddamn funny, Wade Starling!"

In some old photographs of Mama, taken in Arkansas where she grew up, Mama's a slender girl, standing with an ax in her hand atop felled trees. She's wearing flour sack dresses and battered shoes. In those days, she used to tell me, people cut logs out of the woods to build their own houses. And in these photographs, Mama looks strong. Like she could do that. Like she could split a thousand logs and build her own house, all by herself. But in other photographs, photographs taken later the same year, she smiles shyly under Daddy's arm. She's wearing his

Marine Corps jacket with the shooting medals. She's wearing his cap, the shadow from the visor covering her eyes. *Who posed her like that?* I wonder. In the photographs with Daddy she looks weak and small, a fraction of her former size.

From the bedroom Daddy shouted, "Shut up, Beverly!"

And Mama, talking and laughing into a hole in the bottom of the sink, seemed very small. She whispered into the drain, a dark ear she could tell secrets to. "Whew," she said, "That's rich. I tell you what."

Bedsprings twanged. Then Daddy was in the kitchen, thrusting his hand into Mama's dark hair. "Bitch." His mouth twisting.

She arced back. And then she was on the floor, and he was on top of her. It happened so fast. Unbelievably fast. Like human electricity. She said quietly, "Please. Don't. Please." Mama was used to tribulations. They were part of her way of life. But people knowing about them, that would make them *truly* bad to her. And so her voice stayed low.

I ran outside, crawled beneath the trailer, counted spiders. Dug my toes into cool sand. Under this trailer I was safe.

Even now, at forty-five, many's the night I listen as my trailer expands, tightens, breathes.

I love living here in these small rooms.

Most people call me trailer trash. Think everybody dreams of stone houses.

This trailer's only a ten-wide. When Daddy bought it, that was considered big. But a ten-wide is humble now. In a world where fourteen's the norm and twenty-four's preferred. But, then, I like things close. I like to be able to reach out and feel life's edges.

Because what can be worse than a vast and open space? Where anything can be found and destroyed?

I read a story not long ago in the *Scout*. About a man that killed a Canada goose.

One of the world's few respectable birds. When they mate, they mate for life. And when they lose their mate, they grieve. What capacity for love.

The goose nested in a swamp next to a factory where automobile parts are made. In a flatland state, an industrial town. A town where unemployment runs high every time the country must tighten its belt. The factory was going to be shut down.

Each spring employees took their sack lunches outside. Waited for her to arrive. To nest. Hatch her young. Waddle to the bald parking lot for food. I think she was like their poetry.

The man that killed her took a baseball bat where she nested. She nested there in the open. For anybody to see. Although here and there were scattered fragments of wrecked machines she could've hidden among.

Afterwards, people asked him why. Why did he do it? He said he didn't know why.

"How?" one of his co-workers asked. "How with only a child's toy has he murdered our dreams?"

I read how her mate staggered over the factory grounds for days, searching. That a factory worker said, "He looks like a sad man who's missed his bus."

FIVE

Shakespearean fatalism. American tragedy.

I read in the *Scout* how a nephew of Ethel Kennedy's was recently arrested for a murder almost thirty years old. Somebody beat a teenage girl to death with a golf club. A piece of equipment used for fun. Relaxation. Precision and control.

"It's like the Kennedys live under a curse," the *Scout* said.

Some people said that when Bobby died, too. When I saw the train on TV bearing Bobby Kennedy's body away, I cried. Oh, how I cried.

Thinking about his little ripple of hope. About those quick jabs he made with his hands while giving a speech, driving his point home. On the campaign trail, how he reached out to people with his open hands. Or how he often passed his fingers thoughtfully through his long hair. When Bobby died they kept playing that speech on TV, the one he'd made about his brother's assassination. During that speech, Bobby had tried to smile, but death had worn him out. Bobby said, "When he shall die, take him and cut him out in little stars."

Watching me cry, Daddy said it made him sick to see a girl with hormones so out of control. I was thirteen. And Daddy said at my age everything came down to a feeling between the legs.

Daddy hated the Kennedys. He was a Nixon man.

╱ ╱ ╱

Soon after Bobby Kennedy died, a silver tabby showed up on our doorstep looking like bones. Wet from rain, he was lizard-like. I held him. Felt his heart beating raw in my hands. I called him Little Bobby.

Little Bobby sat on our steps all day and all night and cried out for food. He begged so hard that soon all he could make was a croaking sound. First of all, I poured him some milk into a chipped bowl. Have you ever seen an animal weep? I have. Because as he lapped, tears, genuine tears, streamed into the white. I fed him more. I fed him all day. I scattered little chunks of beef and bologna over the yard. A chicken neck Mama had fried. Last of all, a wiener that hung from his mouth rubbery and pink like a swollen tongue.

The next day, under the trailer, the green drone of flies.

"Your goddamn fault," Daddy spat a wad of tobacco. Scooped the bony thing into a shovel. It was horrible, its eyes and mouth open, its little belly bloated from all the food.

Daddy said I'd killed it with kindness. Which is all too true, Daughter. Sometimes you must beware the hand that feeds you.

- - -

I have another cat now. A black one named Spook. She eats with gusto but not from human hands. Won't let me touch her but sometimes hunkers in my lap. Razor claws gripping. She's beautiful and fanged and gleaming. Watching her hunt, I imagine she's forever haunted by dreams of flesh. Of blood. The terrible beautiful gore of chomping off a thing's head.

She smells of bone marrow and cobwebs. Of darkness, moss and mold. Like she sleeps in graves.

SIX

The military police always saluted our old truck as we passed through the camp gate. Civilians weren't allowed. Going through the gate felt like being let in on America's secrets, and this feeling always seemed to put Mama in a good mood.

"Just look at our sweet boys marching," Mama would say as we rode past columns of men in their khakis on our way to the commissary.

I had to admit, under all that authority, they did look sweet-faced.

Watching them, I thought about how Daddy seemed to long for the days when he was a drill instructor at Parris Island. How he seemed to miss all those men hating and fearing him at the same time. It was about control, Daddy'd tell me all the time. You had to condition the men to do anything you asked. Anything. That way, during battle, during the baptism of fire, they could be counted on. Daddy had a variety of punishments. "Smoking?" he'd say. "That's buckets over the head and let 'em smoke all they want." One of his favorite chastisements had to do with shaving. "Guy don't know how to shave clean?" Daddy'd say, his eyes fierce, gleaming. "From then on he shaves from the tits up." Daddy'd always sigh at the end of his telling. He was fed up with the way Vietnam was going. "The Corps is getting soft," he'd say. "That's why we're losing the war."

"Just look at our boys!" Mama would beam. "Anybody tries to mess with our country, watch out!"

Living close to the Camp LaGrange Marines made Mama feel safe.

I didn't feel safe. Mama never read the newspaper. But I read the *Scout* all the time. The whole world on our doorstep, six days a week. I read all about these soldiers' outlaw ways. Fistfights. Robberies. Drunk driving. Rape. Bodies of women found in dumpsters and lakes.

It wasn't safety I felt.

Only thirteen and I was already putting on hotpants and painting my face. Walking to the Gas-n-Go on the corner of Hunnycutt Road and Highway 17 in the evenings when I knew Marines would be on their way to off-base rentals. Waving at their cars.

Loving it when they leaned on their horns. Whistled at me. Screamed. Shouted at me, "Oh honey!" and "Jail Bait!"

A dress rehearsal for my teenage life.

My future was with these Marines, I decided. At thirteen I decided this. There was a need to fill, and I'd fill it. They were part of my destiny. These boys that flew death's planes. Who wore death's clothes. These boys that laced themselves tight inside death's black boots.

Even in the late fall when the evenings took on a chill, I went out bare-legged and walked the road. Shoes snapping dry weeds. Little seeds sticking to my socks. I bent to pick them off.

Back then, along certain stretches of Hunnycutt Road, the pines were thick on both sides. If I walked down the exact center of the road, I imagined, if I walked on the dotted lines, if I held my arms out very straight, and if I stretched my arms until I felt my shoulders straining in their sockets, I'd be able to touch the pine needles on either side.

SEVEN

Daddy searched his whole life for a claim to fame.

He was the first to settle here on Hunnycutt Road. When it was called Route 3. Route 3 was just a dirt road that sucked hard at our truck tires every time it rained. Daddy carved a place for our trailer out of a thick stand of cedars and pines. Ours was the only home on this road for years. A fact Daddy thought should earn him some respect.

But Waterville honored Floyd Hunnycutt instead. Named this road for him. And every time the *Scout* did a story about Floyd, it reminded Waterville that Floyd had pioneered Hunnycutt Road, that he was the one to pave it, the one to build it up into one of the finest residential neighborhoods in Waterville. Second only to those on Country Club Road. This did make Daddy fume.

I was ten when Floyd built his housing develop-

ment across from us and called it Peach Point.
When he built his own cream-color brick house
across the road from us. Always a lover of words,
Floyd would've understood the power of alliteration
and fruit names. *Plum* had already been taken by a
community on Country Club Road, but that
wouldn't have mattered to Floyd. Because as Floyd
would've known, a plum might be regal, cool, even
exotic, but a peach ... a peach is the way people
really want their lives to be. Golden, mellow, sweet.
Kissed by the sun.

Peach Point had asphalt trails Floyd named after
his girls, his wife. Cleopatra Court, Lydia Lane, Nan
Drive, Lenore Circle. Which suggested that all roads
lead to family harmony. An idea people like. All this
Floyd knew.

The Hunnycutts lived in that cream-color brick
house just across the street. I went there all the time
to eat, to watch their color TV. To play Crazy Eights
with Nan and Floyd.

We played in Nan's room. Floyd always sat on
Nan's pink frilly chair, the one with ruffles that
reached all the way to the floor. Floyd was a dark
prince on a pink toadstool. Bela Lugosi without a
cape. Nan and I sat on the floor where Floyd sneaked
looks at our cards.

Floyd congratulated me when I won—I nearly

always won. He called me *honey* and *sweetheart*—
words I never heard at home. I crawled into his lap
like a trained kitten, while Nan looked down and
played with the buckles on her shoes, quiet in her
defeat, accepting. Then she vanished. Or I should
say, though she still sat at our feet, I no longer chose
to see her. It was just me and Floyd.

I was thirteen. Too old for men's laps; too young
for men's laps. One day I'd be in hotpants, walking
down future's road. In girlish jumpers at Floyd's the
next. It was glorious to be a little girl at Floyd's.
Debonair, he'd say, stroking my hair. *Convivial*.
Teaching me to love words. Teaching me to love
myself.

Afterwards, I looked the words up in the thick
dictionary at school. Solemnly turned the onionskin
pages. Smiled as I read the definitions. Our secrets.
Deep secrets. Deeper than the Grand Canyon.

As Floyd Hunnycutt cuddled and stroked, I
rolled my tongue, purred. Sometimes even said
meow. Possibility was a real place. A place as real as
Floyd's lap. As real as his hands.

I wanted to marry Floyd like girls want to marry
their own daddies.

EIGHT

Peach Point attracted people like the Bells. People with nice cars who grilled meat behind honeysuckle-choked lattice. People who used too much starter on the coals. The summer I was thirteen, I was drawn to the Bells' summer weekends by the smell of honeysuckle and gasoline and fire.

Zeke Bell's parents looked like tourists in their own yard. Dee-Dee lounging in a blue bikini under an umbrella, reading thick books she called *sagas*. Her veined feet soaking in a kiddie pool. Clyde wearing Hawaiian shirts and pastel shorts. His skin peeling from too much sun. His red hair wild beneath his baseball cap.

Near their grill was a concrete yard ornament. A duck Dee-Dee called Clyde. Clyde had orange feet and a matching bill, so bright they were like cutouts from some neon pumpkin. The rest of Clyde was white. The kind of white that makes your body throb. That leaves a vibrating image after you've shut your eyes.

Sometimes Dee-Dee talked to the duck. Talked, for example, about Mama-Bell, Clyde's rich mama who lived in Raleigh. "Now Clyde," she'd often say, "you just tell old Mama-Bell where she can stick that will of hers. Somewheres the sun don't shine." Zeke's daddy would pick up a long fork and jab the meat hard then. His stubby toes would clutch hard at his flip-flops.

The meat Clyde cooked was always dry. Tasted like lighter fluid. Burnt inner tube. Animal death.

"The meat's dry," Dee-Dee would say to the duck.

Zeke never commented on the food.

Yes, the meat's dry, I'd think. But I ate all Clyde would give me. Sometimes asked for more. In response, Clyde would throw more meat on the grill.

And the four of us would eat that, too. I ate more than anybody. It was good to eat in the presence of others. With people who didn't scorn you if you left something on your plate. Food being an event people can share. An outcome people can talk about, like the weather.

It was good to eat at the Bells'. At home we didn't eat together as a family anymore. Mama cooked. She left food for us on the counters and stove. Like offerings.

Mama ate while she cooked. Taking bites here and there. Choosing always the boniest pieces. Her failures. Her imperfections. Everything burnt. Everything that didn't rise. Or that fell apart. But I picked out the best pieces I could find. Then hid in my bedroom to eat them. Hunkered over the food like I was doing something shameful. Daddy ate at the kitchen table, a territory he'd staked out. Didn't eat much of what Mama cooked. Preferring his own fare. A case of Schlitz. Smelly things out of cans. Raw onions. Hoop cheese.

At the Bells', Zeke sat in a lawn chair beside the azalea bushes, fiddling with an old radio that bled different stations together like a massacre. The radio was junk. Zeke, the champion of any lost cause. Of which Daddy thought Zeke was one, a lost cause. That kind of boy, he used to announce, always dies young.

Zeke was sixteen; his body was always broken or bruised—attractively. He cruised at high speeds, his Ford Galaxie splitting the air madly. Foomp-oomp-oomp-oomp of Thrush mufflers.

— — —

And it was thus and so all that summer I was thirteen. A summer of dirty sunsets.

A summer of barbecues. A summer of honey-suckle. A summer of dry meat.

Until the day Clyde kept balling up his fist and pushing it into his back while rolling chicken legs around on the grill, saying, "My *back*!" The day he made quick, stupid jabs over the hot fire then groaned and sat on a cedar stump, eating sliced Del Monte peaches from the can. Clyde's skin was especially red that day. His elbows raw, like they'd been scrubbed with sandpaper. His skin erupting.

Dee-Dee had her thick book laid aside. She'd taken her sunglasses off and was rubbing her closed eyes.

Zeke was twisting the knob on the radio. That summer Zeke was forever twisting the knob on that radio. Placing his hopes time and time again in that radio he knew was doomed to fail. The sound coming out of the speaker holes was always thick as blood and confused.

Do you believe me when I say I had a sad love for him? That my love was something akin to prophecy? And that I saw the whole sorrowful arc of his life when his hand was on that knob? Or when I heard the pound and throb of his Galaxie?

Can you believe me? That this is true? This story of my life?

I hope so. Because when others tell my story

they'll use different words. When someday you see my story in the *Scout*, on the back page of section A with the stories about the weird lives people have lived, think about what I'm saying now.

"It's like an *ice* pick. Jabbing, jabbing, jabbing," Dee-Dee said. "Clyde?" She was talking to the duck. The bright duck that wobbled in the sun. "Clyde? Would you please tell my pitiless husband I've got a migraine?" She took a drink from a sweating glass.

"Migraine *my sweet ass*," Clyde Bell said.

"Shut up, Clyde," Dee-Dee said. She meant her husband. "My head hurts!" Dee-Dee's fingers were pressing on her eye. Pressing and releasing. Pressing and releasing.

Clyde speared a peach slice and shook it at her.

This scene plays in my mind like a black-and-white movie. A movie that uses one spot of color for accentuation. Like *Schlindler's List*. Like the little red coat that takes you on a journey toward stupid and pointless death. The peach slice was like that. Fateful like that. Tellingly tragic like that. It held your gaze is what I'm saying. Its color. Its movement. I'm not exaggerating. I'm telling the truth when I say it quivered like it was frightened and alive.

"Your migraine's in that damn glass." Clyde's face was deadly serious. He flipped the fork forward. The peach slice landed on the flat of Dee-Dee's chest, slimed between her breasts.

It was a sorry thing to do. A kind of violence that's done to trust. Dee-Dee covered both eyes like she was playing a child's game. But she wasn't. "Ezekiel, son," she said, "would you please go inside and get me a Coke? A nice Coke to freshen up my glass?"

Zeke's eyes scanned the yard, like he was looking for danger. "A Coke?" He didn't want to leave, I could tell. But he was his mama's son, always doing as she asked. Always getting her whatever she wanted. Drinks, a book, a towel, her sunglasses, a comb. He always fixed her plate before he fixed his own. She never even had to move from her chair.

"Go on ahead, Ezekiel," she said. Her voice gentle. So sweet it touched me.

"And turn off that damn radio," Clyde complained.

Reluctantly, Zeke went, but left the radio blaring. And as soon as the storm door slammed behind Zeke, Dee-Dee, her eyes still covered by her hands, said to her husband, "FFFFFFFFuuuuuuuuu-uckkk Youuuuuu!" She yelled it. Long and loud.

Clyde's face turned stormy. His body swelled. You actually saw anger invade him, inject itself into his whole being. Suddenly, he dived toward Dee-Dee. Both arms before him, legs sprawled. An awkward diagonal dive.

Dee-Dee hadn't expected such ferocity, that was plain. I don't think they fought much hand to hand. Dee-Dee didn't have a look of resignation like Mama always had. No, Dee-Dee's limbs shot straight out and her mouth formed an "O" as her chair over-turned. A gesture of complete surprise and fear. Her body had momentum. She curled into a ball and rolled. Finally striking her head on Clyde, the duck. Dee-Dee's body unfolded. But not in the pretty way love unfolds, not like a moss rose unfolds to the sun. At first she twitched in the grass like I'd sometimes seen dying animals do. Then she was still. Out cold.

In the meantime, Clyde Bell was tangled in Dee-Dee's chair, fighting it while it *click-clacked*, expanding and collapsing around him.

Then Dee-Dee's knees flexed. She pulled herself up and rested on her elbows. "Where *am* I?" she cried.

She meant it. It was a *real* question and not a joke. She said it like she couldn't believe what her life had turned into. That of all the places on the globe, she was here. And how had that happened? I wished I had an answer for her, but her question was much too big. Big as the wide world, for there were so many nicer places she could have been.

"It ain't Disneyland!" shouted Clyde. Flung the

chair off at last.

There'd be no more barbecues at the Bells' for three years.

- - -

Seeing me watch Zeke's Galaxie burn up and down Hunnycutt Road, Daddy'd laugh. "Girls are drawn to a boy like that," he'd say. "Like doomed magnets." The Thrush mufflers *thrumped*. "That boy's wild. He likes that sound. You know why he likes that sound? Do you? Do you? He likes that sound 'cause it reminds him of that throbbing between his legs." Pause. "You know all about that. Don't you? *Don't* you?" When I didn't answer, he grabbed my arm. His face a monument to anger. To disappointment and distress. The fact was, he always despaired he'd never had a boy. A boy to carry on Starling, the family name. Often whined, *Goddamn it, I need a boy. I could do things with a boy. Could get things accomplished with a boy.* "If you get pregnant, goddamn it, if it's a boy, I'll take care of it. I want it," he said. "Goddamn it, it'll be mine."

He'd seen me walking Hunnycutt Road. Probably thought I'd already been with men. And why wouldn't he? I couldn't blame him for that. Because, yes, I was begging for love. It didn't matter what kind. And what he suspected had already happened, would happen. And happen soon enough.

NINE

Daddy was always telling me how dangerous boys were. "Boys are unpredictable," Daddy'd say. One day, he snugged a cube of cheese in an onion wedge and said, "Sit down."

I'd come to understand it wasn't me he was worried about. He took pleasure in passing on knowledge of any kind. It made him feel powerful. And he liked saying things to embarrass or shock me. Enjoyed watching me squirm. This made him feel powerful too. Since I was thirteen, he said, there were lessons he had to teach me. Lessons he said the health ed class at school wouldn't cover.

Mama was in the living room, watching her favorite soap opera. It was her one pleasure in life, she said.

I wondered how much Daddy could add to what I'd been learning in school. The mimeographs from period one health class seemed very complete to me. *Sex drives or urges are normal*, the mimeographs read. *They affect our attitudes and relationships with others. The purpose of the sex drive is for reproduction and expression of love and desire to share in every way with another.*

"A girl can get into trouble," Daddy said.

He meant Stuart. Stuart Deal was Daddy's poster child for the insanity of boys. Stuart, a senior at Waterville High, had recently killed Judith Lamb on their first date, and was now in the crazy house for life. Stuart was a big boy, soft and fat with vast white hands. Hands he'd strangled Judith with.

People couldn't believe it. He'd never been in trouble. He was smart in school, all his teachers said. He liked science—everybody kept saying that—he liked science!

The control of the sex drives or urges shows signs of maturity. The failure to control one's sex drive results in unfavorable social relationships.

Stuart came from smart, quiet people. His mama was a substitute teacher. His daddy an architect and engineer. A month after the trial, Stuart's daddy shot himself with an old-time revolver. But his mama carried on. Once a month she boarded the Greyhound with a pan of homemade brownies for her boy. Stuart's favorite.

"Now you take that Stuart. That's the way boys are. They can't control themselves. If things go too far, well a boy's got to have it. He can't quit. A girl can't say no and expect the boy's going to quit." When Daddy drank his eyes got wild, like a hawk's. An unblinking fierceness.

I thought about Stuart's big, sweaty hands underneath Judith's dress, sticking to her nylons. His inhaling and exhaling, urgent and wet, like a hurricane in her ear.

Sexual intercourse is not a game or a plaything. Maturity is necessary to achieve success. The consequences of heavy petting are severe. The male must experience frustrating feelings and BE ABLE TO EXERCIZE SUPERHUMAN CONTROL.

"That girl let Stuart pet her and then said 'No.'"

The female is far less sexually aggressive than the male.

Making Judith sound disobedient.

Like a dog.

TEN

Back in 1960 when Hurricane Donna came to shore, Daddy left us to endure the storm alone, saying afterwards that, like most women, Donna hadn't amounted to much. But she'd hit land at 95 miles per hour and it'd seemed to me the trailer had rocked so hard its wheels had left the ground. A window had set up a vibration, a loud haunting whine. Mama had come to my bed and lain against my curved back. So near I'd felt her heart throbbing. "Mama," I'd said, more frightened than full of love, "I love you more and more." I'd tried to regulate my heartbeat with hers. My fast, frightened heart to her slow and steady one. That was such closeness.

The day before Donna hit, the sun had sent out a kind of warning. It'd had a weird, dirty glow. The same that summer I was thirteen. The sun looked like that almost every day that summer. The light dirtied everything it touched. It felt like the world was dying.

Those evenings, if Daddy was away, Mama and I would watch Cleopatra Hunnycutt from our kitchen window. Cleopatra, wearing dime-store dresses and black thick-soled shoes, would leave her cream-colored brick house and cross Hunnycutt Road, heading for a little patch of woods behind our trailer. Big Foot and Sasquatch, her classmates had called her when she was in school. She was nineteen now. A graduate of Waterville High. Still living at home, and not working any kind of job. Mama and I watched silently as Cleopatra lumbered past our fence on her way to the woods. Her hair, which she cut herself, fell across her face like a bad mistake. She was always with a boy. A different boy. Always a gawking boy with a paper bag of booze to bribe Cleopatra with.

Cleopatra went about stooped, taking small steps with her arms close to her sides. Unless she was drinking. Then she stood erect, covered a lot of ground fast. Threw her arms out to touch the world.

Sometimes, after Cleopatra had disappeared, I noticed out of the corner of my eye that Mama was watching me. Aiming at me both her fear and her reproach. I felt her shrink away from me, afraid of what had started building itself inside me. Something inside her begging, *Pearl, don't you do that. Don't be like Cleopatra. Don't let that be you.* But she never spoke it out loud. And the more I walked Hunnycutt Road, the more she pulled away.

Eventually she stopped watching me at all. She only looked at the sun.

― ― ―

That summer, I might have lunched with the Bells, but every chance I got I suppered at Floyd's. The Hunnycutts ate at the same time every night. At seven o'clock. Sharp. The stomach doesn't yearn according to a clock. But at least supper was something you could count on at the Hunnycutts'. Even if the meal did have an undertow of misery. Even if it felt like that moment before a tragedy strikes.

Floyd ate in his recliner watching TV. Lenore Hunnycutt never ate, it seemed. Only cooked and served. So I ate with Cleopatra, Lydia, and Nan in the pine-paneled kitchen under a tapestry of the Last Supper. A gigantic wooden fork and spoon hanging on either side of Jesus and His Disciples. As if to say, *Do not eat with your hands!* It wasn't a real tapestry. Just one of those painted rugs Floyd sold at his furniture store. Sometimes at night I'd walk around Peach Point. Looking through windows into the lighted rectangles of kitchens. Almost all of them had the giant fork and spoon sets and the Last

Supper tapestry. It was like both were an unwritten rule of the kitchen.

Lenore was pretty. But she was white and cold, like a hospital. Her whiteness dispersed into the whiteness of whatever was around her. Of walls, of light. By winter, like yesterday's light, or yesterday's snow, like something I thought I saw once, Lenore Hunnycutt would disappear. She'd just be gone. And she'd never come back.

Lenore always sprinkled her preparations with exotic spices she stored in small glass jars. Little dried things like shrunken heads or clipped finger-nails. The jars clinked together in a wooden rack beside the stove like test tubes. But, though she used spices, her suppers always tasted sanitized, bleached. And none of the different foods touched.

At every meal, Cleopatra sat, black hair falling into her eyes. Looking around like a felon. Her family was ashamed. Of the drinking. The boys. The cheap, ugly dime-store clothes when they could afford Belk Tyler's. Always the heavy, black shoes. Nan would speak to me of Cleopatra in hushed tones when we were alone in the restroom at school. "She doesn't act right," she'd say.

Nan and I were the same age, but you'd never know it. She looked and acted like a fussy adult. Even then, Nan wore grown-up clothes. Straight skirts. Blouses that tied in great bows at the neck. Nan was always pronouncing judgment on Cleopatra. Turning red, Nan would tell me, "She spreads her legs for boys."

My nerves caught fire when she said that. Nipples puckered hard under my shirt. Little badges of my shame.

Cleopatra always seemed to be waiting. She wouldn't begin eating until the rest of us had. Then she ate apologetically. Slowly. With thankfulness. The way I imagined somebody would eat their last meal. It was like she was hoping that somewhere between the chewing and the swallowing somebody would put a hand on her shoulder and tell her not to worry. I kept waiting for something like that to happen. For somebody to turn to Cleopatra and say, *It's all right. I love you.*

Every time you finish a meal, it's like a little death. Nothing left to do but push the plate away and wait for hunger again. Watching Cleopatra eat, I sometimes thought about Mama. Couldn't help remembering the winter I was ten and it snowed.

When you live in the South you measure your life by the coming of snows. You'll remember them, every one. They stick in your mind, vivid as political assassinations. In the South, snow is wonder, snow is Camelot. Stepping across it, you gasp as it fills your shoes. But that year the snow was defiled. Radioactivity from the West. The testing of the bombs. "Do not eat the snow," the radio warned. All that beauty. Chock-full of poison.

But Mama wouldn't be cheated. Pleasures were too few, she said, and too far between. And so, with the porch light spilling across the white, Mama bent over the snow in her turquoise raincoat with missing buttons. The only coat she owned. She kept it closed by pressing her arms tightly against her sides.

I could smell the poison. Even after she'd added the milk, the sugar, the vanilla. A sharp smell like the tip of a match. I would *not* eat it. So she ate it all. She was that way. She never wasted food. She cried real tears if she had to throw food out, even the smallest shriveled grape. "When I was growing up in Arkansas, there wasn't hardly anything to eat ever," she used to tell me. "Us kids passed a jar of pickles 'round the table. And the jar went 'round and 'round that-a-way. And when the pickles was gone, we drank the juice." She made a horizontal loop with her index finger to show that the jar kept going around until the juice was gone. A never-ending circle of hunger and gloom. Gloom and hunger. On and on.

I watched her soft throat pull the snow cream down. Burning her blood. Scattering its lethal seeds.

Years after she'd died, looking at photographs of Hiroshima in the *Scout*, the earth blistered and scarred, I knew that inside her body it must have been the same.

She pushed her bowl away. Folded her hands across her belly as if to say, *Time will sort this out.*

By the time I was sixteen she was dead of cancer. People will say I'm crazy. That a person can't get cancer from one bowl of snow. That there are so many other factors ... That statistics suggest ... And so on. And so forth. To them I say, *Quiet. Be quiet for once.* To them I say, *You were not there.*

I remember Mama trembling as she took the last bite of snow. Cleopatra trembled like that, too. At the end of her meals.

Cleopatra would look around, touch the hair that hung over her right eye like a black curtain. Wait. Lenore Hunnycutt would be washing dishes, her shoulders working up and down as she scrubbed pans. Floyd would be reclining in his easy chair, watching the flickering images of war. On a TV tray, his soiled plate, discarded like a sin.

It was Lydia who finally did something.

Cleopatra was the outcast of the family, Nan, practical, judgmental, and plain, the one who always made straight A's. Lydia was the pretty one. Floyd kept photos of Lydia on the TV in a three-piece frame made like a triptych. Lydia's latest school photo, Lydia in her cheerleading garb, Lydia when she was a little girl, holding a stuffed toy she called Wolfie. There were no photos of Cleopatra or Nan anywhere. No photos of Lenore or Floyd. Only of Lydia. Pretty and popular, the trophy child.

Like Cleopatra, Lydia was soon to have her own strife with boys. And then she'd become Zeke's girl. Lydia, just weeks from this moment at the Hunnycutts' table, would swallow a lethal dose of Floyd's heart pills and die.

But this day was Lydia's triumph. This day was Lydia's gift. Because, in a conquering gesture, like the Statue of Liberty, Lydia lifted her fork. She stabbed her meat patty and raised it into the air, fist tight around the fork. She examined its properties. Then she dropped the patty into Cleopatra's plate.

A gift. Maybe a reprieve. What courage. A little more time for someone to tell Cleopatra everything would be all right.

~ ~ ~

After supper Lenore would go to bed and the Hunnycutt girls would join their father around the TV. I always joked there weren't enough chairs in the living room, no place for me to sit, except the floor. Floyd would go along, throw out his arms for me to crawl into. I'd get into Floyd's lap and go to sleep. Thirteen, yes, but skinny, not very mature for my age. A little girl.

The flickering light from the television was a fire. The faraway noises part of my dreams. I wanted him to love me. I wanted him to love me the best. As a little girl, I wanted to marry Floyd. How was I supposed to know better. How? I thought I wanted to marry him. I thought it was what I wanted.

ELEVEN

"No time for talk now," I called to the Pentecostals yesterday. "I've got work to do. Weaving and
tying off my rugs. In a day or two Mrs. Phoebe
Marshburn will be here. For her monthly supply of
rag rugs for her beach store. You know Phoebe."

The Pentecostals said nothing. They weren't out
for idle talk. Chit chat. These people get down to
brass tacks. But they know Phoebe. Everybody
knows Phoebe, Grande Dame of Waterville.

She sells my rugs alongside other handmade arts
and crafts. Wooden ducks. Seashell art. Stoneware
mugs. Watercolors of sand dunes, sailboats, pelicans,
gulls. All at tourist-trap prices.

She labels my rugs "local artist," but I know she
tells customers the scoop.

*The one that had that boyfriend. And they killed
that man.*

That, my Daughter, is why everything I make sells. Most people like the feel of history in their hands. And souvenirs of disaster. They like to touch tragedy and see how it feels. I understand. I collect things, too. Books I find at the Goodwill about the Kennedys. Articles from the *Scout*. All kinds of stories about tragedy, natural or man-made. Keep them in scrapbooks I store under my bed.

Phoebe supplies me with cloth for my rugs. Factory defects. The deceased wardrobes of her acquaintances. The wardrobes of her deceased acquaintances. Blankets and sheets with stained pasts. I cut or rip the cloth into strips and sew them tongue to tongue. Roll the sewn strips into balls. Feed the strips onto mahogany shuttles and weave.

I have books. *A Handweaver's Pattern Book* by Marguerite Porter Davison. *Key to Weaving* by Mary E. Black. *Handweaving: Designs and Instructions* by Lotte Becher. In them are patterns I want to try. Patterns with names I like to say at night before I go to sleep. "Young Lover's Knot with Twill Border." "Wondering Vine." "Sea Star." "Anemone."

I've got plans is what I'm saying. I've got plans.

I look through the books again and again. The pattern drafts are beautiful. They look like music notes. Sometimes, when I sit at my loom, I feel like I'm at an organ. Pumping pedals and making music that could go out to nobody but God. If there be a God.

For now, working with these rags, it's a simple tabby weave does best. Over, under, over, under. A simple tabby, the most primitive of all patterns. Before you know it, you've turned rubbish into something people can use. And you did that. You did it with your own hands.

- - -

I've only shown my loom to one person, a boy that worked summers for Phoebe. A college boy that majored in art at East Carolina University. Graduate school. Brian Lily. He told me he paints pictures. But not seascapes or tobacco barns. He paints naked people. Nudes. In the manner of the Renaissance. He glorifies the human body. Because he believes the human body is holy. Is divine. I was thinking he had a lot to learn.

He came a few months ago to pick up rugs for Phoebe. Innocent face. So much like an angel with that white skin and curly red hair that in spite of myself, in spite of my distrust of the kindness and goodness of people, I let him in. Damn it, I let him in.

And can you believe it? He touched my loom like he loved it. My Leclerc. A loom with battle scars from so many years of use. It was used by sol-

diers back from World War II, I told him. "Therapists," I said, "found weaving has the power to heal.
It healed me." I'd never mentioned this fact out
loud. This simple fact that seemed so striking to me
now. Then I thought, *What Phoebe must have told
him!* Maybe warned him about me before he braved
the trip alone to see the crazy woman who weaves
rugs for a living. Who spent two years at
Hollingsworth Home for Troubled Girls. Then I put
the thought away. I adjusted my floppy-brimmed
leather hat. "I've been weaving on this loom right
here in this trailer for nearly thirty years. Twenty-
seven to be exact." My voice had a certain gravity,
then. A weight I liked.

"I've read about that, weaving as therapy." His
eyes sparkled, like moonlight on ice. "Where did you
learn? At Hollingsworth?"

That Phoebe! "No, after." He looked confused.
Probably thinking I'd been in another institution as
well, learned there. So I told him how I'd found the
loom at 'Nam Sam's, the military surplus. How it was
in a heap of strange parts. How I asked for instructions, and the cashier said, "That's your problem." I
told Brian Lily how I'd written to the Leclerc company in Quebec. And instructions arrived in the
mail, in French.

He asked me if I knew French. I told him I

didn't. That I'd used the pictures in the instruction booklet. I took the booklet out of a drawer, saying, "Look." How to explain it? Saying this simple word, this invitation. You have to recall, I'd not made such a solicitation in years. I offered the booklet to him, for him to hold. But he chose to move next to me. Held one side of the instructions while I held the other. It felt like sharing a hymnal. I said, "See?" I felt something opening in me. My goodwill was pouring out of me, filling up the room. "It says, *Pour ergotherapie et readaptation.*" I read the note, type-written by one of the descendants of the Leclercs:

> *Miss Starling, Sory I do not have any more the english version of those therapeutic looms. We work in close cooperations with the military re-habilitation programs, mentals hospital, and centers for peaples who had accident. Around 1948, we shiped looms on 88 diferent military bases for the U.S.A. government. Please excuse my poor english writting. Its a foreing language for me.*

I pointed with my finger to *Mentals hospital. Peaples who had accident.*

"Interesting," he said. "That you're self-taught." And then he loosened the booklet from my grip and laid it on my loom bench. Stood waiting. As if to say, *What more can you show me?* He was in no hurry.

So I decided to keep showing him things. In truth, I wanted to. Wanted to feel his breath stirring the hair on my head, my arms. He was so interested, so kind. I felt like I could puddle at his feet, like water. "It's something about the motion of the hands and arms," the boy began, talking about therapy again. Rowing his own hands and arms like he himself was weaving. Moving his hands and arms in a way that respected weaving. It looked like a devotion, the way he moved. "It's like babies," he said. "What they do as they lie on their backs taking in the world. That repeated gesture of bringing the world into themselves. Like this. See?" He did the motion. And I lost myself in it. Felt like I'd fallen into the motion of his hands. He kept bringing them to his chest in that slow way. "See how it's like what babies do?"

"I do see." But I was sorry I'd spoken, because he stopped then.

He touched my loom again. It felt like he was touching me. And he knew this. For next he started paying great attention to details about the loom. Touched the painted logo. Rubbed his fingers over it, feeling how the logo is slightly raised from the surface. "Leclerc. That company goes way back, doesn't it?" He was smiling, looking at me.

"1876."

His smile broadened, and he looked at the loom again. "Well, that's a great loom." He looked at it admiringly. "And four harness. You could do some complex designs."

I went to my shelf, pulled down my pattern books. Books it'd taken me years to collect. I showed him. Told him my plans.

His attitude shifted then. He shrugged. "These are nice designs," he said, glancing at the book. "But these patterns, they aren't art, really. Following patterns, you see, is more of a craft." The word craft sounded low the way he said it. Like something beneath doing. "You ought to take classes," he said. "Create your own designs."

Now, I thought, *I can hate him*. Yes, that old familiar feeling. Who'd he think he was? College boy.

But then I saw Brian Lily bent at the knees, his hands going into the intricacies of my loom, into the strings, the heddles. He pushed one of the treadles down with his hand and watched with interest as the harnesses changed position. Harnesses one and three up, two and four down. He pressed a different treadle. Now, two and four were up, one and three down. Just as it was supposed to be. No doubt, he had to delight in the fine balance of my loom. How the action was smooth. He did like it. He really did. And I couldn't hate him, not then, not with him doing that. And not with him rubbing the wooden parts, the maple timbers. Like you would a cherished pet. Or something wild that for some reason lets you get close. Like a deer that's just come up to you in the woods.

This boy's hands and arms stunned me. He was just the age when veins pop out in the hands and arms, as though the body can't hold its suspense. Inside, it's all hot blood, rushing and moving through the excited halls of the body. And the body can't contain its excitement, no.

It'd been a long time since I'd felt that excitement. So many years dedicated to the simple motion of this loom.

"You've done a beautiful job of stringing her up," he said. *Stringing her up.* A picture flashed in my mind of me and Brian Lily, purely carnal. I should've been ashamed. "I've seen where the warp gets so twisted in the back," he continued, "that the strings break." *Yes*, I thought, *bodies do get twisted. Broken.* "There's no sense in that," he said. *No*, I thought. *No sense at all.* "But yours is perfect." *Mine is perfect.* He touched the warp strings softly, fingertips following the strings from the back beam up through the heddles, through the reed, up to the last rag strip I'd beaten back for the rug. "Perfect," he repeated. "The best I ever saw." He touched the cloth, but looked straight at me. With his eyes he told me, *That's the cloth you've brought toward your own body. Toward your own heart.* The same thing I'd told myself hundreds of times.

TWELVE

I won't say I haven't thought about it. Someday I'll tell you. There are things that should be said to daughters. There were moments I wanted an end to you.

I understand them, I think. Those girls that secretly birth in bathroom stalls, dispose of the baby. Then return to the party and dance, dance, dance.

There were times when none of this was real.

It's real now, oh yes. And as I sit at my loom making rugs and spread my legs wide to make room for my belly full of you, I know this—

You can't be as small as those baby books claim.

One night, not long ago, I dreamed about your birth. You were a red moon slipped out from some dark corner of the sky. A real piece of sky I could hold. It made me want to forgive the sky. For both its calm betrayal and for its frightful storms.

My dream made me want to forgive the sky. A little.

That's right, I said, Drink it in. Your life. The air.

Use your own mouth to tell the world what you want.

PART II

ONE

So, yes, yesterday, I told those Pentecostals, "I've got serious work to do." I gave them the heave-ho.

"Very well then," the old one said. "We shall return tomorrow."

"Whatever floats your boat," I said. And left the window. Sat on my loom bench, blood swooshing in my ears. They can be imposing sometimes in their affirmations.

Daughter, I didn't tell them the truth. Didn't get to the crux. To the deep and wide of things. Beginning with my name. Because what's more telling about a person than their name? When the Pentecostals were here, I didn't say, *My last name's Starling. But I've never had a fondness for those birds. Sometimes they cover my yard, a blanket of screeching tongues. Nothing about their songs their own. All manner of squeaks and whistles they've stolen from other birds.*

Sometimes they even bark like dogs.

I should've told them that. Shouldn't I have? Shouldn't I have said these things?

And when they come back, shouldn't I tell them I prefer the silence of fish to this prattling world? The way fish regard their world without blinking their eyes? Shouldn't I say, "I like carp, who tolerate drought. Who bury themselves in mud while other fish quiver and die. And there, in the dark, patiently wait for the world to flow about them again." Beneath all that muck, something. Flesh hearts, waiting to be revived.

And shouldn't I say, *It's none of your damned business who the father is!* That would feel good. Very damn good.

Should I tell the truth? And if I did, would they believe me? Would they understand?

Oh, you Pentecostals. Is this how you think I planned my life? Don't you think I'm sick of all this tragedy? Of all the dark roads I travel in my sleep?

TWO

Less than a week after Lydia had triumphantly raised her fork and given Cleopatra the meat patty, Cleopatra was thrown out of Floyd's house. Daddy and I watched from our kitchen table, Daddy eating oyster crackers and Limburger cheese. I was waiting for Mama to fry the chicken.

That day Daddy's life looked like the bent chair he was sitting in. Had the very fragrance of what he was eating. The slippery hope of the shows he watched on TV. Game shows that promised instant fame. All day long he'd been repeating facts he'd learned on game shows. Which he did when he was in a dark mood. He was in a dark mood because lately everywhere he looked, there was Floyd. On TV, doing commercials for Furniture Circus, *The most fantastic showroom on Earth*. On billboards standing beside Maytag washing machines. My *showroom won't take you to the cleaners!* In the *Scout* as "Businessman of the Year."

Did we know what an onager was? Daddy asked. "An ass!"

Onager. It was his favorite word after that.

And he asked us, did we know about the cockroach? It went all the way back to the dinosaurs, he told us. Face glowing red hot, as if with God's own knowledge. He smiled as he smacked on his cheese. Said, "The roach will outlive us all!"

Which was to say success is fleeting. Even Floyd's.

Mama's view on the roach was much more basic. "Wherever there's roaches, there's a reason," she said. She was wiping a counter with a dishrag, getting ready to mix batter.

"Hunnycutt never would've made it in the Marines," Daddy said, his eyes narrowing as he studied what was happening at Floyd's. "He says he's got a heart condition. Heart condition, *my ass*." He made little sucking sounds, cleaning off his teeth. "Well, some people go their whole lives not knowin' they're a coward. That's why a man needs a war or two." He thought a while. "That's why there *is* wars."

It'd grown dark, the sky full of clouds. Lightning streaked across the sky as Cleopatra ran around and around the outside of Floyd's house. Screaming. Something like, "Oh Daddy, what are you gonna do now?" The words were garbled and frantic, like turkey sounds.

"What's going on over there?" Mama cried out, stepping away from the hot grease to look out the window. "It's so cloudy and dark! What's she mean, *What are you gonna do now?*"

"Who the hell *knows?*" Daddy yelled back. "That girl's crazy. That's not what I was talking about anyhow. I was talking about *Floyd,* goddamn it!"

Cleopatra banged on a window and somebody in Floyd's house, somebody I couldn't see, snapped the blinds shut. And then all of Floyd's lights went out. Cleopatra sat on the grass in the rain then, and wailed.

I'd heard of untamed cats to live in gopher holes, but where did a grown person, a castaway like Cleopatra, go?

To Paradise? Yes, to Paradise. A trailer park on Highway 17. A place called Paradise because it so obviously isn't.

A few months after Floyd threw her out, Cleopatra had a live-in boyfriend and a baby. A little girl she named Breeze. One day, from the school bus, I saw Cleopatra. Sitting in the black, sour dirt at the front end of a trailer, digging holes with a fork, planting packets of seeds. It was a warm winter day.

The bus stopped to let off a rough little fifth grader named Clovie Hill. I thought, *Cleopatra. Nobody plants seeds now.* Somebody in Paradise was listening to "In-A-Gadda-Da-Vida." It was loud, so everybody in the bus, everybody in the trailer park was listening to "In-A-Gadda-Da-Vida." The sound distorted by cheap speakers.

"Don'tzzzzzz know thazzzzz I love ya babzzzz. Don'tzzzzz know thazzzzz my heart zzzzzbe truah!"

Paradise is that kind of place.

I watched Cleopatra. Planting seeds in winter. Once they sprouted, they'd never survive.

~ ~ ~

Clovie moved away and our bus didn't stop at Paradise anymore.

During the next two or three years, Cleopatra had two more babies. Boys she named Thaddeus and Flavian. All her kids had different fathers. But Flavian's father stayed. And he married Cleopatra. And adopted Thaddeus and Breeze.

When I was eighteen, just after I'd gotten out of Hollingsworth Home for Troubled Girls, I was eating a hamburger and fries at Buck's Grill. Customers began whispering behind their newspapers. I heard low mumbles in the kitchen, words settling on the food, like soot. They were talking about me.

"*Something, something* that girl."

"*Something*, just out of Hollingsworth."

"*Something*, killed that man."

And then I saw them coming up the sidewalk. Cleopatra's whole body was swollen, splitting like a big tree. Some sickness she had. And Flavian pushed her up to the door in a twice-big wheelchair. Cleopatra wouldn't fit through the door. So her husband Flavian and their little kids came into Buck's, ordered "To Go" and took the food outside.

And all of this was funny to the people at Buck's. Gathering at the window to look at Cleopatra and her family, they couldn't believe their eyes. It isn't many times you see something like this. A person too big to fit through a door. An entire family eating on a sidewalk that isn't meant for eating. "This ain't no sidewalk café," a customer said.

The waitress barked her laughter. Two greasy men put their hands to their mouths and hissed like tires, their faces turning dull, bloody red.

They all laughed. And laughed. And laughed. That's because they didn't see. They didn't see how the family all gathered around Cleopatra as around a table, Flavian and Flavian and Thaddeus and Breeze. Standing, they ate their food, the kids softly and curiously fingering the shiny wheels, the handles, the foot pegs, Cleopatra's hair, her messy arms. They touched the splits and cracks on her big legs, exploring the way a baby does its mama's new face.

They touched her like that. Like they were babes. Or like they were happily blind.

Through the years, it seemed like wherever Cleopatra was, whatever Cleopatra did, her family all gathered around her sweetly and tenderly. Nudging her ever so often, like fat bees.

I see Cleopatra, sometimes. Flavian still pushes her chair. From his uniforms I can tell he's worked at places like Mike's Car Mart and Jiffy Lube. Each time, he nods his head toward me like he knows me. He places a hand on Cleopatra's shoulder and slows the chair down. Cleopatra opens her mouth like she wants to tell me something. The chair almost stops. And then she looks away. Flavian puts both hands on the chair handles and soon they're out of sight.

The day Cleopatra had to leave Floyd's house, Daddy turned away from her agony, his fierce hawk eyes locking onto mine. "That girl ought to be beat 'til the piss runs down her legs," he said.

As if to say, *Just thirteen and look at you. You're turning out the same way.*

He toyed with his cheese, clucked his tongue against the roof of his mouth. Then cleared his

gummy throat. A sound that signaled his pure disgust. Of me. Of everything. That sound indicated I
wasn't worth punishing. I wasn't even worth talking
to.

He was eating Longhorn cheese now. "Bought
Longhorn," as he liked to say, "by the half hoop." He
liked the way the words came out. Half hoop. Like a
marching cadence. *Hut, Who, Hreep, Whore*.

Mama had no comment. She gave all her attention to the chicken she was about to fry. I watched
her, almost jealous of the way she rolled the meat in
the seasoned flour in a most tender way. That's the
way she was with food. Always gentle.

The grease crackled loudly as the cool meat slid in.

THREE

One of Lydia's and Zeke's classmates, Gene Shackleford, brought a magazine one day during lunch period that he wanted to show to as many students as possible. Gene ironed the glossy page with his fat sweaty fingers, leaving streaks. "Check it out!" he said. All excited. With the proper awe he thought a magazine like *Famous Hot Chix* deserved.

It was a picture of Jackie O., naked beside a swimming pool. A helicopter shot taken while moving. With a long-range lens. It could have been anybody. But we all believed. Needed to believe. And we all hated her. For marrying the ugly Onassis. For surviving that awful day in Dallas. Parading around in that blood- and brain-spattered dress. *Who did she think she was?*

How unkind I was to survivors then. Thought it was stinginess at the root of their survival. Your sympathy belonged to those in the ground, I thought. The living were wallowing in the gravy of extra years.

Daughter, it's easy to love the dead. Complicated loving the living. All those messy demands the body makes. All the questions the living force us to ask ourselves.

1. What would I have done? Stay in the car to whisper last words or save myself like Jackie did, crawl out shamelessly on my hands and knees?
2. What's an ear? A channel like a drain, taking in words until we become fat with secrets and lies? Or if we're lucky, maybe love?
3. How did Jackie feel as she sat alone, watching reruns on TV of the casket being drawn away. Did she think about that? The last words she didn't say? The poverty of that flag-draped box?

FOUR

In September, a north wind shook the still-green leaves off the trees. Waterville felt like deep winter for three brilliant days. Everywhere people's gardens took on a wild, tangled look. Then shriveled and died. Mama threw blankets and sheets over her zinnias, saving the flowers for a few more weeks.

At the football game against Swansboro, I kept getting whiffs of mothballs. Wool sweaters exhumed from chests and trunks. The cold had everybody supercharged. Girls laughed at the electricity in their hair and kissed boys on the lips. Players bloodied their opponents' noses. Coaches demanded broken bones. Mass murder. Victory. "Kill 'em," the coaches yelled. "Eat 'em raw!"

After Gene Shackleford made his second touchdown, he swooped Lydia Hunnycutt from the sidelines where she'd been prancing back and forth like a beautiful blond horse. Lydia tucked her legs under Gene's arms, pressed her feet against his back and threw her arms into the air. A gesture of complete surrender.

They looked like one person, one body. Celebrating. But after every celebration, the plunge. Jubilation's fuzzy aftertaste.

Now Gene followed Lydia all around the school. Once, I saw him pinning her against the lockers after school as she struggled to get her books out. His big neck pulsed and he clawed at his own shirt.

That past summer they'd put Stuart Deal in the crazy house in Raleigh for life. Gene looked like he might be just as crazy. At the trial they'd asked Stuart again and again, *Why? Did Judith say something to make you mad? Did she make fun of you? Did she hurt you, son?*

No. No. No.

Then why?

I don't know.

I thought often back then about how Ida Deal must look. Her pinched face behind the glass in the Greyhound, watching tall pines of rural towns give way to concrete and glass and big city complications. The brownies on her lap, sweating under plastic wrap.

- - -

The county still paints animal silhouettes on its school buses. Believing children are too dumb to read numbers. A cat. A bird. A bear. A bunny. And Grand Lake is still a place of black water, skunk, and lichen.

Grand Lake is where the bunny bus was parked on a Saturday afternoon two weeks after the Swansboro game. Just about everybody got a kick out of that, the bunny bus. You kept hearing it at the lockers and in the classrooms. *The bunny bus*. And always the laughing. The student that'd been assigned the bunny bus was Paul Darlington. A senior who'd been driving that same bus for two years. Somehow Gene convinced Paul Darlington to hand over the keys.

Inside the bus, Lydia had sex with Gene. And three other boys from the football team. "Animal love," everybody said. "In the belly of a bunny."

It never was clear who caught them. Even the *Scout* never got a handle on that. Paul Darlington's parents, some said, made him tell where that bus was on a Saturday when it should've been parked in the Darlingtons' yard. But that's not what matters. This matters. Says much about the public mindset—the students' sex acts might not have seemed so bad. Might not have had the same suggestion of an altar being defiled. Might not have been covered so extensively in the *Scout*. Or caused the same public uproar. Except they happened in a bus. Which is state property. Getting the whole county, the whole state of North Carolina, involved.

All the students were suspended for three weeks. To their houses, to their parents' wrath.

This matters: I thought Lydia's problems started here. In concepts simple as "bus" and "lake."

— — —

First day back from suspensions, Gene stripped off his shirt at lunch. Showed off his scabby back. Stretched it out before anybody who cared to look, like a magazine. Gene could draw a crowd. More than a dozen of us looked on as he said, "Where my old lady beat me. With a coat hanger." Gene had the thick body of a man. But his face was smooth and soft, like a baby's. His back was fat. Skin poured over the sides of his Levi's. He'd have scars.

Then his lips twisted. "The bitch." I didn't know whether he meant Lydia or his mama. But his words shocked me either way. Girls hid astonished smiles. Guys laughed nervously, hyena laughs.

Later that day, I saw Lydia in the second floor bathroom. Alone. Silhouetted against a tall window. Dabbing big purple bruises on her legs with Cover Girl. Lydia, the pretty one. The one who'd tried to save her sister. Who'd put the meat patty on Cleopatra's plate.

FIVE

Waterville Senior High didn't have a cafeteria then. Just vending machines. Cold sandwiches or hoagies for the toaster oven. Hostess Cupcakes, Little Debbies, assorted chips. Snowballs, Twinkies, Moon Pies. Food you can't imagine has ever been touched by human hands.

"They're sending her to Hollingsworth," a girl named Robin said in the sandwich line one day.

At first, there'd just been the whispering. Amazement of it all. Then girls tripped Lydia in hallways. Nan said she'd seen boys taping porn to Lydia's locker. Poking messages in Lydia's books saying things like *The Phantom Lover*. Or *Slut*.

"No shit!" Moreen cried. Before, it was just whispering. Now people shouted Lydia's shame.

"Oh my God," Candy, Moreen and Robin's friend, said. They were like the three witches in

Macbeth. Always together. Not quite destructive. But drawn to destruction. Fascinated by it.

But Lydia would never be sent to Hollingsworth, a place where you either fell in line or you died. A throwaway place for throwaway girls. Drug therapy. Shock therapy. She died before they had the chance.

That October, people along the coast prepared for Hurricane Gladys. Boarded up windows. Stocked up on flashlights and food. Waterville, ten miles from the coast—as the crow flies—was on alert, too. I spent time wondering what it'd be like at the Bells' or at the Hunnycutts'. How they'd wait out the storm. Wondered whether they'd sit together or deal with their fear in separate rooms. But Gladys snubbed us. She marched on by. Mama sighed with relief. Daddy celebrated at Saigon Sal's. But I felt hesitancy. An inner pressure; an inner fear. Like we hadn't quite escaped.

Meanwhile, more and more, Lydia's blond hair hung in limp strands, and her eyes were two black holes that could swallow a person whole. Zeke, champion of the hopeless, hardly let her out of his sight at school. He was always gliding Lydia around like she was something on wheels. Stroking her back. Fine-tuning. Touching with utmost care. Even so, she shrank into herself like hot plastic.

He'd stop then. Speak something sweet in her ear. Pass his hand through his hair, swiping it to the side. Like he wanted to see her better. Bobby Kennedy had swiped back his hair, I remembered, during the most thoughtful parts of his speeches. That same gesture. The one Daddy hated so much— *Damn longhair*.

One day at lunch, Nan whispered, "I hate Zeke." She was pawing at her elaborate hair. She'd been experimenting with old movie star hairdos. Different kinds of twists and buns.

I said, "Why do you hate Zeke?"

"He calls Lydia all the time, every night. He begs me to give her messages. Lydia likes Zeke but I won't do it. She can write his name in her schoolbooks and listen to sad songs, like 'Is That All There Is?' all she wants to."

I thought about what Natalie Wood said in *Love with the Proper Stranger*, a movie Mama and I had watched at the Iwo Jima theater in Jacksonville. That love wasn't something you fell into like a hole in the ground. But it looked like Zeke had. That once he'd looked into Lydia's eyes, he'd fallen right in. Deep into the bottomless wells of Lydia's black love.

Lydia's dark eyes reminded me of a little girl's named Henrietta who'd sat at my worktable in the first grade. Henrietta was so skinny. So full of sleep. Little bones stuffed in a wrinkled dress and tramped-down shoes. I remembered how I'd watched her dream. Wondering if her visions were as wild as her black, thorny hair. The teacher whipped her for sleeping, as the class looked on. Later that day, I ventured to the rims of Henrietta's eyes. They were like two dry wells. I was drawn to them as to stony tombs. Do you want to know the truth? I envied her. The same way I'd always envied all the dead children I'd ever heard or read about. Those green ones who'd crossed over to the other side.

Henrietta didn't look away from me that day. I looked away. Afraid.

The same with Lydia. Since the bunny bus, Lydia wasn't the same. She knew dark things others didn't know. Dark things I wanted to know. I didn't want to look away from Lydia's eyes. I couldn't tell Nan about my fascination. She'd never understand.

Nan slipped a bobby pin from her hair and rummaged it over her scalp. Said, "Daddy forbids Lydia to talk to Zeke. Lydia needs to get her head on straight." Nan's teeth were rigid, like a ventriloquist's.

By now I was mad. Nan's value system! The way she accused, judged. She'd said she hated Zeke. I wanted to say something. Something heartless, like,

You look stupid with that hair. Anger boiling in my chest, I barely resisted saying that. But I did tell her, "Maybe Zeke's trying to help her." Then added, "For all *you* know."

"No he's not!" Whispering loudly now. "*You're* the one that doesn't know anything! Zeke and Lydia are having *sex*! Did you hear me? S-E-X. That's supposed to help her? How's that supposed to help her? That's what got her into all this trouble in the first place!"

How'd she know? How did Nan know Lydia and Zeke were having sex? Had she seen them doing it? Or was it something she saw afterwards, something quieter? Like the light of some long-extinguished star. Or the echo of one person passing through another.

"I'm *never* going to have *sex. Never! Ever!*" Nan declared.

I believed her. I didn't know. Didn't know there are grown men who do it with little girls, even their own. And Floyd was one of these. Didn't know that on my fourteenth birthday, Nan would wait until Floyd had left the house, then sneak me into his bedroom, where the two of us would kneel beside the bed. And I'd think for a crazy moment, *Nan's going to pray.* I didn't know she'd reach up under the bed and say, "Look here." That dozens would slide

toward us, like a wave. Not *Playboy* women with cat-
tish eyes and airbrushed skin. But girls that looked
cracked open. Wounded. Broken, sliced, axed.
They'd spread themselves out in front of the camera.
Spear themselves with their own fingers.

I didn't know that Nan would sob and ask me,
"Do you understand now? Why I'll never have sex?"

A lie. Because by this time Floyd had already
brought her down. And before that Cleopatra. And
Lydia too.

I didn't know. That Lydia's problems didn't start
on the bunny bus. They started with Floyd.

SIX

Lydia died in late October, just before Halloween and not long after Hurricane Gladys traveled up the Atlantic into oblivion. I wondered if her death was what I'd felt coming. If that was why I hadn't felt soothed about the hurricane's chosen path. Lydia's story was on the back page of Section A, where they put all the oddball news. Stories too weird to believe. Those stories about fetuses wrapped in plastic bags. Bizarre electrocutions. Women scalped by industrial machines.

At thirteen, it had me wondering: *Are some lives worth more than others?*

It was just one paragraph. Telling how she was found face down on the floor in the kitchen by her sister, Nan. A dark pool of vomit on the linoleum beside her head. How her daddy said she'd been distraught over some boy. A boy he didn't name. He didn't have to. Everybody knew it was Zeke Bell.

From that day I've told myself over and over, *Let Lydia stay dead, let her.* But no. Even now in this new millennium I sometimes hear her. See her. Imagine the pool on the floor where her stomach tried to empty the poison out. Remember how she tried to save her sister with the meat patty. And I know she's part of my own wet heart. That she'll always be. That I'll always dream about her. Dream her flawless and dream her bruised. Dream her soul purple and crushed. She's in my blood. Paddling through my arteries and veins, calling out, "Halloo, Pearl, where *were* you?"

Lenore and Cleopatra didn't go to the funeral, held in the Bonecutter funeral home chapel, in business since 1924. A family business that'd now passed down to two unmarried middle-aged brothers. Their chapel was the best in Waterville. It had red velvet drapes and white cherubim on each side of the curtain rods. Floyd wore sunglasses so nobody could read his eyes. Nan sat beside Floyd with a bloated face. Her eyes swollen, two wounds. I thought of the boils Daddy'd once had on his leg. Remembered how he'd taken a knife and cut the sores himself until the yellow sickness ran out. "Maybe Lenore and Cleopatra weren't *allowed* to come," I heard a neighbor, Lucille Gore, speculate.

As they shut the casket, Nan wailed. A choked yodel that would've sounded funny at any other time. I made fists in my lap. Imagined plunging knives into her eyes. So deep only the black handles showed. Her eyes would explode, I imagined. Bleed. Daddy'd always spoken of how blood cleans wounds. The body heals itself, he'd say. No need to ask Jesus.

Mama and I sat with the neighbors. Clyde and Dee-Dee Bell. And Lucille Gore, who lived close enough to the Hunnycutts in Peach Point to see all their doings. Six Waterville businessmen sat in the middle of the chapel. Crows in slick black suits.

Then, in the very back, Moreen, Candy, and Robin. They kept putting their hands to their mouths and funneling chatter into each other's ears. Rocked on their bony rumps. Tugged at their short skirts when their garters showed. Legs were long and gangly. Like baby animals. Fawns in black hose and high-heeled shoes they couldn't yet control.

When Zeke arrived, Candy shrieked. She'd always been loud and had no manners at all. "Oh my God!" she said. It was her favorite phrase.

Moreen liked Zeke. You could tell. She took a metal thing from her purse. Put her fingers into the scissor-like handles and used it to curl her lashes.

Zeke sat up front. Alone. Close to Lydia. He wore a baseball cap turned backwards. A neon orange T-shirt and big-legged shorts that went down below his knees. Bright beach clothes. Bold colors for somebody already thinking about bold moves.

Clyde shouted across the chapel, "You look like a goddamn clown!" Then he looked around to see if anybody would absolve him for having such a sorry boy. Dee-Dee massaged her forehead. Another one of her headaches, I guessed.

"That ain't right," Mama whispered. I think she meant Zeke's clothes.

Somebody whispered loudly, "He didn't have to come."

Gene Shackleford was not there.

─ ─ ─

As everybody gathered for the graveside services, Lucille Gore cornered Mama and me against a mossy tombstone and told us what had happened. She said Lydia was with Zeke in his Galaxie. "He'd parked it right in Floyd's driveway," Lucille said. "Then Floyd pulled her out of the back seat of that Galaxie and she was butt naked." She told us Floyd had beaten Lydia with his belt all the way to the house. "She was running for all she was worth!" Lucille said.

For all she was worth.

"'Course you know Floyd beat her all the time," Lucille continued. "Well, you know he had to. You can't blame Floyd. There wasn't any other way to make that pretty girl behave."

Daddy had never beat me. Yes, he'd talked about it, but never seemed to care enough to carry it through. "You know why this girl's out of control?" he'd say. "'Cause I ain't here every day to kick her ass!"

"Seems like she would've *learned*, don't it?" Mama said to Lucille. "I can't hardly believe that girl done all that." All that. I think she meant sleeping with boys.

Lucille shrugged. "Seems like the more he beat her, the more she strayed. A shame that pretty girl couldn't behave." Lucille said Zeke had threatened Floyd, saying, "I'll *kill* you."

Moreen, Candy, and Robin got out of Moreen's yellow Volkswagen Beetle. They wobbled in their heels toward the Bonecutter canopy, holding their skinny elbows in their hands. Black shoulder bags beating hard against their rumps. They'd gathered close to Zeke. Tried to look sad.

Later, Mama commented about it. "Stupid little tramps," she'd said. "What were they trying to prove?"

But I was wondering something else. What the Bonecutter brothers had thought as they'd washed and prepared Lydia's body. That most intimate part of Zeke still on her thighs. The marks from Floyd's belt on her soft white skin.

- - -

The first night Lydia was in her grave I tried to sleep. But this trailer has always magnified sounds. That night, I heard everything. Needles trembling in the pines. Mama's breathing. The ocean, miles away. Its coming in and its going out.

I thought about Lydia underneath the ground. Wished her face and hands would shrivel like bacon, her body grow leathery under her clothes. Rather than the way it really is. The way I'd read about it in books. The slow rot. Growing long whiskers of mold and staining the pretty silk lining.

I knew that night that her hair and nails still grew. Her white teeth were still hidden behind soft lips. But all her secrets were shut tight in that mahogany box.

She had run for all she was worth.

What had it been like for Lydia on that bus? That's what I wanted to know most. Because I still believed there was something mystical, something wondrous about love. Even love on a bus. In a dirty aisle or on torn seats. Even love beside a dark lake. The bus parked there like a giant yellow fish.

- - -

I walked to the graveyard a couple of weeks later

at dusk with a handful of Mama's zinnias. I just had to see if it was really true. If she was really in the ground. The zinnias were tough and freckled, threatening to go to seed. Zeke was at Lydia's grave. And at the exact moment I saw him, I couldn't help it, it was greedy I know, but I started thinking. If Zeke was drawn to tragedy, then fine. Then what about me? My life? My tragedies? Lydia'd had her troubles. But didn't Zeke know I had plenty of my own? That my life was no bushel of peaches? He should've tried to stay at my house some, I thought. With a daddy that drank and used fists or the flats of his hands to keep Mama in line. Who sat and ate and sulked. Who embarrassed me with his ugly talk. Then Zeke would know. Zeke could be drawn to my problems, I reasoned. Just as well as he had been to hers. If only he just knew.

Zeke had shaved all his hair. He was wearing camouflage clothes and dogtags with no name. He kept rubbing the stubble at the back of his neck and seemed to be in deep concentration.

I put the zinnias at the base of Lydia's stone. Somebody had spray-painted *Slut* in red across her name. I could tell Zeke had been gouging at the paint with something, a sharp stick or maybe a key, trying to get the paint off. "It's got to be Gene or those other boys," I said. I'd seen them huddled sometimes at school, whispering and laughing. I told Zeke I had an idea how bad he felt.

Then he said to me, "You don't understand."

And that hurt. That he believed there were conditions of tragedy I hadn't fathomed yet. To think he saw me, at thirteen, as just a kid. I wasn't. I understood the nature of deep things. Dark things.

I knew he didn't want me to, but I kissed him anyway. Full on the mouth, just as I'd always wanted to do. Our lips were dry and cracked. Misaligned. Unmoving. Pressed against each other like two wounds.

He pulled back and licked his lips. "No," he said. Then he cleared his throat. "Don't you understand? I could have saved her." He sat down and leaned his back against Lydia's defaced stone. Then in a low voice full of self-disgust, "I should just leave."

I should've been glad he wanted to leave. To break this tie to Lydia if only for a little while. This tie nobody but him could break. But I didn't want to leave. I sat with him and took his hands. Squeezed. Thought, what wonderful devices. What a miracle, his hands. How rare. What power for curing. This is what hands are for. Why they were designed. As engines for concern. If anybody could've saved Lydia, it would've been Zeke. But something about Lydia had been way too broken to fix.

We both leaned against her stone. It was early evening. The moon steered across the sky. Below, the dead sighed. And now I knew. This was the best place I'd ever been. The best place I'd ever be. Somewhere between death and everlasting time.

"I'm old," I said. "Already old."

He put his hand to my chest. Pressed, as though to stop blood.

I'll never forget how that night we rode. Traveled country roads fast, snaking through the dark. He turned off his headlights and gunned through intersections. I understood why. The small orbit of his headlights, it was too confining. With the headlights off, it was like he was moving fast. Free, under black water. I understood because I'd always liked the feeling of darkness, of blackness, of water. They had blurry edges that helped me align myself with the world. He ignored stop signs. Roads rolled out before us, ribbons of black.

I wasn't afraid, only mindful: Others had collided at these junctures, on these roads.

"I understand you," I wanted to say.

That night, we went into stores. First, a country grocery. Where Zeke pressed his thumb into a Hostess cupcake. I smashed my fist into a Moon Pie. We drank orange sodas in plain view and didn't pay. Then to other stores. Where we fingered goods. I poked holes in paper sacks, letting food spill out. Tried on lipstick. Zeke took bites out of candy bars and put them back on the shelf. Finally, we both went into K-Mart and tried on all the shoes. By the end of the night, we'd been run out of a dozen stores.

And no matter where we went, Zeke opened all the doors. He ushered me inside. He steered me out. He touched my back tenderly as I crossed each threshold. He put his arm around my shoulders as we walked to the Galaxie, but he didn't lean on me roughly to support himself the way I'd seen other boys do. His touch excited me. His touch said, "You matter." His touch said to me, "I would never hurt you."

As Zeke took me home, tears sprang into my eyes. I sniffed and ran my sleeve across my nose. I leaned my head against his window, and, to my shame, my hair left a greasy streak. I tried to clean the window. Pulled my cuff over my hand and scrubbed. Then I thought about Mama, always scrubbing, always trying to keep her surroundings clean. About how much she hated dirt and grime. As though her unhappiness would be compounded by a dirty house. Like mother, like daughter? I wondered, was this all life had in store for me? *Leave it, Pearl. Leave the window alone. Reach inside yourself for bigger things, why don't you?*

Zeke was quiet, rubbing his head with the flat of his hand. All his energy, all his capacity for love seemed used up now. I watched pines stream by the window. Mournfully thought, *This is the last time you'll be with him like this.*

Even so, I knew what people would be thinking, saying—she's Zeke's girl. I wanted them to think that. *She's Zeke's girl now.*

- - -

Lenore Hunnycutt moved to some kind of spa. A place in Chapel Hill for nervous wives called Whispering Pines. Cucumber slices on the eyes. Massage therapy. Gentle counselors on the premises. A place not at all like Hollingsworth.

After Lydia died, I didn't eat at Floyd's for a while. Then on my fourteenth birthday, Nan had me over to share the little cake she'd made, and, as I've already said, to share something else. The magazines under Floyd's bed.

I suppered at the Hunnycutts' regularly after that, just Nan and me at the table now. Floyd still ate in his chair, watching the nightly news, watching images of a war that might never end. At first, we all ate sandwiches, or carryout, or Nan warmed up food from cans. Then Nan bought a cookbook called *Foods We Remember* and got serious about preparing our meals. Dishes like Tuna Touchdown. Super

Duper Cheesy Casserole. Fancy Soufflé Surprise. Salad Extraordinary.

Each recipe included wisdom: *When nature made her lovely plan she gave to woman the care of a hungry man! Anyone liking music with their meals should drink their soup! When God made the primal paradise, a garden He fashioned! Now, every spring, man steps toward his Eden with every seed he plants! Do not underestimate seasonings! Careless measuring means failure! Discouragement!*

I started excusing myself from their table in the middle of meals. I'd go into their bathroom and shut the door loudly for effect. Then sneak out and go into Floyd's bedroom or Lydia's. Just to look around. To see and feel their belongings. I knew it was wrong, knew Floyd didn't want anybody in these rooms. What else do closed doors mean? My visits to these rooms felt dirty, like a lame obsession. But this feeling didn't stop me, no.

Lydia's room looked just like she'd left it. Her clothes still hung in her closet, still held her form, like the moltings of shimmering bugs. At the end of her bed on the floor, a pair of bikini panties, no bigger than a girl's fist. Your uterus, I remembered the health teacher saying, is about this big—holding up her fist.

Your womb. It could have power, I'd thought

when teacher had done that. Power like a fist.

On Lydia's dresser, a toy, her favorite. The lewd wolf with a rubber face, mouth open, licking its lips. Wolfie.

Floyd's room always smelled of leather. The smell so strong I imagined it had weight. That it thickened near the floor. In his closet, a long row of shoes peeked their toes from the dark. A dozen or more belts were threaded onto hooks by their shiny mouths. Sometimes I took a belt down, slapped it softly against the palm of my hand. Against my arm. Against my thighs. Then I'd hit myself harder. At fourteen, I thought about punishments and what they mean. Knives and belts. Banishments and locked rooms.

Punishments had to mean love. They took thought and diligence to carry out, didn't they? They existed for good reasons. Why else would somebody go to all the trouble of creating them if not to make things better? If not say, *You are precious to me*. No, Mama and Daddy never punished me. What was I supposed to think about that? I thought about that a lot. I reasoned I was no longer worth their while.

SEVEN

"You ain't gonna believe this," Daddy told Mama. "But some guy out in *California*, some *writer's* asking questions about Steve McQueen. Wants to put me in his book. His book about Steve McQueen!"

"You and Steve McQueen?" Mama said.

"Yeah," Daddy said, his head already in his closet, sandwiched between hanging clothes.

"The movie star?"

His muffled voice. "Yeah, the movie star. 'Course the movie star. Who else? Onager! Damn!"

At the kitchen table, Daddy flipped through a photograph album. Muttered every now and then, "Not that one, goddamn it" or "That's not the one. *Hell!*"

"What are you lookin' for?"

"Goddamn it, Beverly, shut up. Shut up before I

rip this thing all to ... There it is! Platoon 53. Get my glasses, goddamn it."

Mama handed Daddy his glasses. He put them on in a hurry, then studied a group photograph. "Nah," he said. "Not him. Where? Right there! That's goddamn Steve McQueen."

"Steve McQueen?" Mama squinted at the photograph.

"That's Steve McQueen. Hell!" He was breathing hard. "Don't you get it? *I* brought Steve McQueen through boot camp." He stabbed his chest with his thumb. "Goddamn Steve McQueen!"

"You did?" Mama asked. Uncharacteristic of her, showing doubt about something Daddy'd said.

Daddy threw his hands up in annoyance. "Looks like you could be more damn excited for me," he said. "That's what I hate about this family. Nobody in this goddamn family's ever excited for me. Nobody's ever on my side."

"I always liked Steve McQueen," Mama said, trying to be on his side. "His characters always had good names. Like Rocky or Max."

"Beverly, what the hell does that have to do with *me?*"

Mama blinked. Realized something. That Daddy was right. Liking Steve McQueen's characters didn't have anything to do with Daddy. Nothing.

She kept blinking like a machine doing compu-
tations. What she'd said had nothing to do with
him.

She said, "I liked that movie *Love with the Proper
Stranger*." Blink-blink. "With Natalie Woods. Me
and Pearl saw that. At the Iwo Jima."

This also had nothing to do with Wade Starling.

Daddy frowned and slammed his fist on the
table. "Is that a Western, Beverly?"

"No." *This has nothing to do with you.*

"Well, he only played in Westerns, damn it."

Mama turned and started scrubbing the kitchen
sink. Talked to herself. Talked into the drain. "That
part where he says, *I'll* kill *them before I let them touch
you!* He said that to Natalie Woods. It was about
abortion. That wasn't no Western. That was set in
modern times. That was Steve McQueen. *I know it.*"

Daddy cleared his throat, signaling this was the
end of the discussion. She could shut up now. It
wasn't worth it to hit her or to knock her down. He
was off into his own dream.

He leaned back in the kitchen chair with his
hands behind his head. "Yeah, I'm startin' to
remember stuff now. He was a goddamn trouble-
maker. Yeah. Tough keepin' that ole boy in line.
Yeah. Yeah. Without a doubt, that boy has recollec-
tions of Old Starling," Daddy said. "You can bet. Up

in that Hollywood mansion, he *remembers*. Yeah. He remembers me! Yeah. He remembers me all right."

Later, under the trailer in the cool sand, I thought about it. Women in Steve McQueen movies wanted to be treated nice. That's what Suzanne Pleshette said in *Nevada Smith*. "Just treat me nice, Max. That's all I want." But in the end she spurned him. Chose to die out in the swamps alone. And Natalie Wood. She said the world didn't come to an end every time one pair of lips touched another.

And that's true. In the end, McQueen did what the women wanted, not the other way around.

I thought, *Steve McQueen. Damn Steve McQueen!* We'd never hear the end of it now. And Daddy'd be shouting it at Saigon Sal's—"I brought Steve McQueen through boot camp! Goddamn Steve McQueen!"

Some woman hanging off his neck, squealing, "Oh wow!"

＿ ＿ ＿

That book about Steve McQueen came out in all the bookstores. Daddy bought one and looked through it a dozen times. But he wasn't in the book anywhere. After this discovery, he bought a case of Miller instead of his regular Schlitz. Instead of his stinking things, instead of tuna, salmon, and sardines, instead of hoop and Limburger cheese, he

THE SECRET OF HURRICANES

bought breakfast cereals. Bright boxes. Pretty shapes. Sugar-and-honey-festooned. Mixed with fruit. Marshmallow hearts, moons, and stars.

"How could that writer just skip over boot camp? A major part of McQueen's life?" Daddy whined.

"I don't know," I said.

"Hell, I didn't just influence McQueen. I made McQueen." He took a big gulp of beer and made a bitter face. "Champagne of bottled beer, my ass."

I noticed then how much Daddy was like Clyde Bell. They were from different worlds, but they were just the same. Daddy grew up poor. Traveled the South and the West looking for jobs when there were no jobs. Had his appendix ripped out by a dentist in a dark boarding house room. Fought two wars. Had bad dreams. Sometimes at night he gasped. He lunged out of bed and tried to climb the curtains. His senses racing like missiles. While Clyde had always had things soft, his life cushioned by family money. Old Mama Bell's.

"Reminds me," Daddy said. "You know what an onager is, don't you? Don't you?"

They thought alike. Acted alike. Talked alike.

They ran things. Ran people. It was like God died and left them in charge.

Daddy's disappointment at not being in the

book made him lash out at Floyd. He made sucking sounds, cleaning his teeth. "An onager! An ass!" His bowl full of golden O's. "Maybe that girl did swallow those pills," he said. Making the sounds often between words. "But Hunnycutt's hands ain't clean neither. No sir. Ain't clean."

- - -

I've looked at the photograph of McQueen and Platoon 53 many times. McQueen doesn't look like anything special. He isn't even good-looking like some of the other boys are. He looks brittle from too much Carolina sun.

EIGHT

Mama covered her mouth now when Daddy was at home. As though to keep from saying something she might regret. And when he was gone the hand came off. And when she wasn't watching her favorite soap opera, she talked to herself. Talked and talked all day.

One day she said, "I want just ten good years. Just ten."

She was thinking of life like a race. And since Daddy was ten years older he should finish first. Leaving Mama to do whatever she wanted. "It seems only fair, doesn't it? Doesn't it?" she wanted to know.

Ten years to do whatever she wanted.

But what did she want to do?

"Mama, what do you want to do?"

"Well, I don't know."

"Don't know?"

"I haven't completely thought it out." She scrubbed the counter.

Like I told you, she was always scrubbing something. A thing can only get so damn clean.

"First off, I'd get me one of them gazebos."

"I know you want a gazebo, Mama. But what do you want to *do*. *Really* want to do?"

"Besides the gazebo?"

She'd seen a gazebo on her soap opera, and people with names like Nina and Cliff were always meeting there to fight and to love. Ah, but mostly to love. Mostly to love.

I tried to see the woman that'd felled trees, could build houses.

"It don't matter. I'll never get them ten years," she said. "He'll never die. He'll be here even when all the roaches are gone."

Silence. Scrubbing.

Asking herself the questions that scare human beings the most.

What did I lose?

How did it feel?

NINE

You find a need and you fill it, saying goes. Then you can never be disappointed in your life.

Just after I turned fourteen, Zeke's parents sent him to Raleigh. To live with old Mama Bell. Punishment for stalking Floyd. It was for Zeke's own good, I heard a lot of people say. Ever since Lydia died that boy was a loose cannon, they pointed out. Even the *Scout* printed a story about it:

BELL STALKS HUNNYCUTT
"It's all over love," Hunnycutt says,
"Boy's mad!"

"That boy's obsessed," Mama said.

Daddy glanced at me, and then away. The briefest admission that I was even there. "Time and distance," Daddy said, "might save his ass."

Maybe so. But Zeke was gone. I had hours to fill. So I found a need and I tried to fill it. The pen pal program at the U.S.O.

My letter ended up on a bulletin board in a mortuary at Da Nang and was answered by Sp-4 Albert Oswald. His only letter began: "Sorry I haven't written. Your letter has been on the board for two months. But I've been pretty busy lately."

Pretty busy lately. I imagined so. The death count was announced every day in the *Scout*.

"Call me Butch," he said. "Everybody calls me Butch."

He was from Philadelphia. Of his hometown he wrote, "It is pretty messy there, but such is life."

Butch said he didn't mind handling the dead. Except at night. "Then," he said, "it gets kind of creepy. Sometimes the bodies shift. And they make sounds."

I'd read about that. Bodies groaning and letting off gas. I'd just finished *The Diary of Anne Frank* and *Survival in Auschwitz*. I wrote back about iron gates and Zyklon-B. Nazi tales. Black hearts.

I knew things, I was trying to tell him. I wasn't a child. And I wasn't afraid. That's what I was trying to get across. I was brave. I understood the nature of everything deep. Everything dark.

"I've thought about it a lot," I wrote. "How I am

touching the paper that you have touched. And you have touched the dead. All those boys. Those bodies that have suffered terrible harm."

TEN

At fourteen, I figured out what it was made people drink.

I drank whiskey with Victor Darkangelo and Tobias, two soldiers I'd met while walking on Hunnycutt Road. I drank with them at a sorry place in the woods you got to by following electric lines. An old sawmill. A place where a boy once died by falling through a sawdust pile and suffocating in the hollow center. Sawdust generates heat. Burns from the inside out, leaving all within airless and black.

Tobias was tall. A skinny green bean from Hamlet, Mississippi. Not quite right in the head. Was slow. Not very smart. Like a big dumb child.

Was Tobias his first or last name, I asked him, and Victor snickered.

No other name than Tobias, Tobias claimed. First and last.

"Tobias Tobias," Victor pronounced.

Tobias said his daddy thought a different name like that would carry him far.

Tobias Tobias was a bank robber. He liked to call himself that. Lying on his back in the woods and studying the clouds, he'd say the words "bank robber" like a prayer. He stole a safe one time, he told me. Put it in the back seat of his car. Disguised it with a coat and hat like he'd seen once in a cartoon. The judge gave him two choices. Jail or Vietnam.

A week before Tobias Tobias left for Vietnam, he said he was scared. Cried real tears into my little breasts. Laid me on the ground as one lays out the dead. With reverence and care. Said, "Come *own*, love me, I *love* you."

My belly burned. But I liked the way the whiskey made me feel. All supple and blended in. I couldn't tell where I stopped and the ground began. The world.

I heard Victor Darkangelo somewhere. Saying, *Goddamn. Goddamn. Goddamn.*

⸺ ⸺ ⸺

The letter from Tobias Tobias came a month after I'd seen his name listed in the *Scout,* among the names of the dead who'd been stationed at Camp LaGrange.

Perl,
Sent I did not have enything to do rite now I decided
to rite you.
Just to see how you was doing? I no I am stu-ped. So
if you have enything aganst stu-ped men you don't
have to retern this letter. Ok.
I no what I took form you that day. In the woods. I
took evrything form you. I no you was a vergen.
Darkangelo told me. I jest want you to no, if there is
enything I can do for you, jest ask. And if you have
a babby, I will take good kare of it. I will take good
kare of you to. Perl.
I promess I will not teech it to be a bank robber.
Senserely,
Tobias Tobias.

Albert "Butch" Oswald, I thought. *Take good care*
of this bank robber. He paid for all his crimes.

ELEVEN

When Victor put his arm around me at the snack bar at the Orb Roller Skating Rink, or when he skated too close, or nuzzled my neck in the shadows, or weaseled his hand up my blouse, I expected Floyd to explode. Not to beat me like his daughters, but to make some kind of strong demands for us to stop. But Floyd would only say to us, "Watch out."

Floyd owned the Orb. Collected the money himself from behind a glass partition. I slid the money through a small opening. He took the money. Tore off a red ticket and slid it to me through a narrow slot. A neat little exchange. A personal transaction. Between me and Floyd.

Air currents swirled behind the glass. Drafts that would snatch the ticket unless I held on. And oh how I held on. So there was that moment when both our fingers were on the ticket at the same time. Our fingertips would be on that little red square. That ticket that said, *Admit One*. Mine and Floyd's.

- - -

Victor Darkangelo was from Paterson, New Jersey. I once looked Paterson up in the *World Book*. It's a city of origins, a city of rust. A city of poetry, silk, and guns.

After skating, we'd go parking. He'd play his radio loud. He'd turn it up louder when he heard a song with lots of drums. Like "In-A-Gadda-Da-Vida" or "Moby Dick." Sometimes he danced wildly in front of his headlights. Beating his chest. Slicing through the air with his knife. Sometimes tossing his knife at trees.

His red Mustang was an altar. Sacred beads and crucifix on the rearview mirror. Plastic Virgin Mary glued to the dash. Holy Bible in the back seat. In his glove compartment a holy card with his dead twin sister's picture on it. She'd died of a burst blood vessel in her head when they were just sixteen. Regina looked just like him. Manly and with the same teeth. Narrow pointed ones.

I wondered what it could be like to have a male counterpart. Somebody that looked just like me. Out there sticking it to all the girls.

Victor had a tattoo on one of his arms. A blurry

little cross with his initials underneath, VD. A non-professional tattoo. Done by some friend in Paterson. It looked like a bad skin disease. Victor once said, "Some guy, some dude gave me shit 'bout my initials, man. VD. I took care of it, man. I got *connections*. Ain't nobody ever seen that dude since." Unblinking fierceness. "If you get my picture."

He also had a masterful tattoo of Jesus on his other arm. Rays emanating from His holy head like a lightbulb. Bare chest without those troublesome nipples. No little badges of shame. Instead, a pricked and bleeding heart, its center in flames.

Victor, like Jesus, was a man burning at his core. Being with Victor made me feel close to heaven. Like there were bigger realms. Dark symbolisms that might explain life. New words. *Infallible. Immaculate. Indulgence. Limbo.* A man that religious can't be all bad. That's what I thought.

Ever since I'd seen *The Ten Commandments*, I'd stopped praying to God. That movie made me think God was too old. Too angry and set in His ways. He was always in a bad mood.

Victor prayed to a woman—an idea I liked. A woman could understand a girl's problems, I figured. Her hungers. Her mistakes. *Mary*, I prayed. *Listen to me. You understand a girl's lament. I know you do. Forgive me for saying. But both God and man have passed between your thighs. It's in the Bible and no secret, after all. What can you teach me about love?*

Victor and I had rituals. His knife taking just the tiniest layer of cells. A delicate scraping against my thighs or neck. A purification. Sometimes he pressed harder. Maybe drew beads of blood. Maybe took thin slices. Carved down to the smooth second layer of skin. So delicate, so pink.

It led me to my own fascination with knives. I found a little pocketknife among Daddy's riffraff things. Held the blade against my own skin as I prayed.

Mary, mother of God. I'm being opened. Peeled to my core. What will my lover find? An ocean? Crammed with treasure and bones? Is he a diver? Searching? Spreading his arms and legs—and mine—wide?

Victor and I would have sex next to his car, on an old pink electric blanket. The heating elements and wires within the blanket left marks across our backs. After the gasp had escaped from Victor Darkangelo's throat, after his skin had tightened then released over his bones, he'd fall away from me. Fold the knife. Say, "Baby, I don't want to hurt you." His knife. It left shiny scars, like burns.

TWELVE

Victor gave me a pair of earrings for my fifteenth birthday. Earrings I couldn't wear because my ears weren't pierced.

"So what, you take a needle and you poke it in. How hard is that? I mean, you take a needle and you heat it in the fire, and you poke it through your earlobes. How hard is that? I mean, damn. How hard is that?" He pulled up the sleeve of his T-shirt. To show me the black ink under his skin again, the tattoo he got on the streets of Paterson. "You see that? I mean, we did this in an alley." He looked at the tattoo. Approving of himself. "VD, man." Put down his sleeve. "And, man, you can't even poke a couple of holes in your ears. I mean, shit, it's ears!" Pounded his steering wheel. "You're worried about your ears, and I'm goin' to the 'Nam! Viet fuckin' Nam!"

Elbowed his car window and shattered the glass.

⁓ ⁓ ⁓

So I pierced my ears. A needle, some thread, a potato at the back of the ear. Hundreds of girls have done it.

I put the needle to my lobe. Felt myself moving toward myself. Like if I touched the mirror my hand might go beyond the glass.

Finished. Both lobes strung up, swollen, red. I touched the glass.

"It's a fuckin' celebration!" Victor said later, when he saw my ears. "Goddamn sonofabitch! Does it hurt? Don't hurt, does it?" He swatted at one of my ears.

"Jesus, Victor," I said. My lobes throbbed. They were ugly things, these earrings I'd forced through the swollen holes, blood red glass attached to cheap metal posts.

We were eating hamburgers and fries at Buck's. So named for the moth-eaten deer head that hung above the coat rack. The clothes hanging on the rack looked like discarded shells of people the big antlered buck had eaten. "Hey, Pearl, check it out," he said. "Gotta pen?" I gave him a pen. Victor drew lines, dots and squiggles around a ragged hole in the Formica tabletop. Now the hole was between a woman's fat thighs. She had a rolling belly, gigantic breasts. A stupid head, mouth open, O-shaped. I clamped a napkin over my mouth. Felt my food go sour. "I don't think you like my artwork," Victor said.

- - -

I knew Victor Darkangelo had other girls. Older girls than me with big hips and breasts. Girls he bought expensive gifts for. Bracelets, rings, chains, crosses. Flashy and holy testaments of his love. But he didn't want me to be with other men. Fact is, when Victor thought about Tobias Tobias, when he thought about that day in the woods when all he could do was say *Goddamn, Goddamn, Goddamn*, the Jesus on his arm went into a spasm of rage.

He didn't trust me. Sometimes Victor drove to our trailer late at night. Shined his car lights into my bedroom window like searchlights. Wouldn't turn them off until I went outside.

"Just checking," he said.

"Checking?"

"On you," he said.

"Why? I'm fine!"

He said, "Checking to see if you're fucking around on me."

"I'm not!" However, at such times, everything I said sounded like a lie, even to me.

Mary, I later prayed. *I put love before all. Like you. So tell me. Love. Is it just another way to die?*

- - -

For a whole week after Victor had celebrated my pierced ears, he didn't call and he didn't visit. He didn't harass me in the night. Then I got his letter. He wrote:

Dear Pearl,
I'm in the brig for assault. And it looks like I'll be here for thirty days. They say I beat the guy up. That's a lie. I didn't beat him. I choked him. What are you doing? Just checking. I know you wouldn't fuck around on me!
Love, VD

Victor Darkangelo. He'd be in the brig for thirty days. Thirty days. Thirty days to do whatever I wanted. But what did I want to do?

I painted my face. I put on hotpants that looked like the American flag. A little white shirt, a gauzy thing. See-through and open in the back. And I walked. I walked until a Marine picked me up. And then I rode. I made smalltalk and rode, and asked him to take me to the Orb. He said he would.

He told me was from Texas. That he was a Baptist.

"Ya know," he said, "you oughtn't to walk out late and take rides from people ya don't know. I could've been an ax murderer."

"Maybe I'm an ax murderer," I said.

He laughed in a Gomer Pyle way. "You're joking. You ain't got an ax."

"I don't joke." I took my little riffraff knife out of my pocket, I don't know why. "'Course, it ain't no ax, but ..."

He laughed that laugh again. But he was nervous now. Licking his lips and fingering his steering wheel as he drove. He glanced quick at a *Jesus Saves* sticker on his dash.

"It's so warm tonight," he said. And he was right about that. The car seemed to glide along on a blast of warm air. "You'd never know it was winter. Guess that's the Southeast though."

We turned into the parking lot of the Orb. For the first time I noticed how the streetlights made people standing in the lot look bloodless. Some were huddled close together, like for warmth, but it was in the high 60s that night, with a soft southerly wind.

He hadn't noticed the X-Rated outdoor theater, the Starbright, across the street, and that a movie was playing right now on the big screen. Eventually, enough people would complain about the Starbright that a high fence would be built to block the screen out. But for now the people of Waterville could see some amazing things from the parking lot of the Orb.

"What's your name?" I asked the Texan. I put away my knife, and he looked glad about that.

"Me?" he said. "I'm Tex."

"No, your real name."

"Well," he said, "my real name's Corwin."

"Corwin?"

"Yeah," he said, like an apology.

"You ever watch dirty movies, Corwin?"

"What?"

"Dirty movies." I pointed across the street to the Starbright. "You can see the movies so easy from the parking lot of the Orb. Look." I said, "Don't worry, Corwin. It's just the Starbright, showing naked bodies doing what naked bodies do."

"Good Lord!" he said about the images of a man taking a woman from behind.

But Corwin wasn't all so holy. He kept watching. Yes, he did. He kept watching like a hungry man.

Corwin's head was turned away from me, looking out his window. At the movie screen. Just a sliver of his face showing. A fingernail clipping, almost. His face sloped away exceedingly from the cheekbone. Skull-like.

We're all so alone, I thought. *Trapped in these thick skulls.* This thought kept stabbing my brain. It was like a dull blade plunging in the darkness. It surprised me when it happened. I punched his head. I punched it so hard with my fist. I felt bone against bone. I felt his skin split, and mine. Saw blood. "Pay attention to me!" I yelled. I heard him gulping, swallowing air to rid himself of the pain. "I don't want to hurt you!" I said. "I'm sorry, Corwin. I don't have time to mess around." I'd never hit anybody before. And haven't since. I don't know what made me think I could do that. Except I was like a downed powerline that night, disconnected and crazy.

In one brisk move, he wiped his mouth on his sleeve, and, turning to me, looked blameworthy. Like he'd let God down. He was so skeletal. So close to the grave, it seemed. "What are you doin'?" Corwin was sweating. Big beads on his face. Big dark loops under his arms. "What are you doin'?" His body heaved under his shirt like a stingray I saw one time, in its death throes on a bloody wharf. "Huh? What are you doin'?" Face folding, collapsing on itself, a face trying hard not to cry. His voice, a squeaky-wheel sound.

"You're a purty girl," he blurted out. "A purty girl," he said, desperately, as I opened the door and let myself out. He said this like his life depended on it. And mine. He looked straight ahead through the windshield and gripped his steering wheel tight. "But you could be purtier. Oh God," he squeaked.

"You could be purtier if you smiled."

— — —

Bruce Baggott was a regular at the Orb. He rolled his Camels in his T-shirt sleeve like a '50s bad boy. Bruce had been to Vietnam. Planned to go again. He liked it over there. Called it Disneyland. Wonderland. Called it freedom. He'd killed. Maybe even raped for his country. But looked squeaky clean with his blond hair. With his straight white American teeth. Girls liked him. Talked about him in the bathroom at the Orb, using exclamation marks. He was *hunky*! they said. He was *beefy*! He was *on the edge, man*! He could toss them around *like dolls*. That's what they said. But I imagined being with him would be more like being in a storm or in a war. Like being swept up in something beyond your strength. It'd be something you gave yourself over to, like fate. Forgetting about the past. The future. Who you were wouldn't matter. Whether or not you survived would be out of your hands.

There was no end to his girls. And he always took a different one home. Notched his bedpost. Literally, I heard. Or he simplified things. Took a girl behind the Orb and afterwards put a new sticky star on his skates.

I'd heard from the girls at the Orb that Bruce Baggott just couldn't get used to civilization again.

For instance, they said he always forgot to pay his electric bill. So girls said they had to feel around in the dark at his place to keep from tripping over his weights. Nothing cold to drink, they said, no cups or glasses in the cupboards. So they closed their mouths over the tap and let the water pour in. They took cold baths, I heard them tell each other, and he took them home, still wet.

When the last of Corwin's taillights had disappeared, I told myself to forget it. Oh yes, it hurt me knowing what I'd done to that poor boy's head. My heart was raw and peeling just like the hand that'd struck him. And my belly churned sour remorse until I belched disgustingly. Still, wasn't it time that I got on with my life? I wondered, *How long do people have to hold to their mistakes?* So I walked over to Bruce. He was standing by himself under a streetlight, smoking. Watching the Starbright's screen. The images of a man taking another woman from behind. And then he took another. The man on the screen spilled his seed over the women's hunched backs. Bruce nodded at me as he lit a fresh cigarette. Not too excited to see me. He'd seen me with Victor here at the Orb. But Bruce didn't know my name. He wasn't big on getting to know you.

Indifference. It tormented me then. That's why I went with Bruce behind the Orb. I imagined that place to be like the dark side of the moon. Like the back of your eyeball. In reality, it was hard dirt. It smelled of mammal dregs and leavings. Disappointment. Stupidity. Despair.

- - -

I straightened my clothes. Combed my hair. Brushed off my scuffed knees. I spat in the dirt like I'd seen men do. I gathered myself together, and I went into the Orb to skate. At the window, Floyd made a quick study of me, then, for the first time ever, chose not to take my money. He tore off my ticket, placed it on top of my quarter and dollar bill, and slid it all toward me.

That night, as always, our fingers touched at the ticket counter of the Orb. And in some uncommon way, I thought I sensed sadness in him. All his losses. Cleopatra and Lydia and Lenore.

Floyd brought my rental skates. White leather, criss-crossed with wrinkles. Laces tangled and wild. Tongues lolling. He put them on the counter.

"You look different," he said.

I knew that already. I felt it. Like something inside me was erasing itself. I thought of Lydia's eyes. Were my eyes that deep in my head? And that black? Did I really need to smile like Corwin had said tonight?

"You don't look so well, Pearl. You look sick. You

look tired."

Floyd had always looked like a vampire to me. Pale. Calculated. Slicked-back handsome. A little wild in the heart, as nightfeeders are. I'd always been drawn to him. Why wouldn't I be? I'd felt starved all my life. Fascinated by death and punishments of all kinds. Bela Lugosi loved all his victims. Sank his teeth delicately into their necks. Sucked their blood slow, like sweet milkshake from two straws. Killing them gently sometimes took days. Weeks.

Suddenly, I did feel sick and tired. Just like Floyd said. The skates on the counter looked sick and tired. And all the skates behind him on the shelves. Old. Worn out. Sick. Tired. I felt old. *Already old. Like the Earth*, I was thinking, *weary of its population*.

I put on the skates. Circled the skating floor. But it was oblong, like an eye wide open and watching. The music was too loud. Too much like raised angry voices. So I rolled over to a bench. Lay down, my feet heavy in the skates. Closed my eyes. Thought, *Victor. Pacing his cement cell. Plotting all manner of revenge against anyone who's slighted him. Even me*. All Victor's favorite movies were about revenge, like *Outlaw Josey Wales*. "Ya don't haveta bury a murdered body necessarily," Victor would tell me. Then he'd quote, "Buzzards gotta eat. Buzzards gotta eat, baby, same as worms."

Victor could kill me. Would that be so much out of his normal affairs? It wouldn't be, I figured. Right then, on that bench, with the roar of skates' wheels in my ears, I decided I didn't care. It didn't matter what Victor would do. It didn't matter if he killed me. Or what he'd do with my body, either.

Dying wasn't bad, I told myself. There was a time I could've died, I remembered. Even almost died. I thought about that. *Dying isn't that bad.* I meditated on that. I said it over and over in my mind. *There's a time I almost died.*

Nan and I were just twelve when we got caught in the undertow. Waves lifted above our heads like cobras. The water, all swoosh and roar. People just dots of color on the faraway sands. A wave took me down, and I sucked the water in. This was drowning. It wasn't what I'd expected. Not at all. Not suffocation. Not the slow burn in the lungs. Instead, all silence and ease. A letting go. Or what it must be like before you're born.

The wave sawed forward and back. I found bottom again. Choking and coughing, Nan and I got back to shore, where a lifeguard was crazy and pacing. "Didn't you see the buoys?" he yelled. "Didn't you hear me blowing this whistle? I was just getting ready to come after you. What's the matter with you girls? What the hell's the matter with you?

— 132 —

Are you stupid? Are you stupid or what?"

Nan wailed. Like she always did when things got rough. I hated that. "I'm never going in the water again!" she screamed. "Never! Never! Never!"

My meditations on death that night at the Orb had put me in a kind of trance. I remember trying to lift my feet. But the skates were too heavy. "Take it easy," Floyd was saying. He touched my forehead. "She's got a fever," I heard Floyd say.

I heard a girl's voice, "I thought I should tell somebody. I mean, I thought she might be dead or something!"

"Oh, she's not dead," Floyd said. His voice a tranquilizer. *Debonair*, he used to say. *Convivial.*

"She's just a little tired. That's all."

"I'm okay. I'm okay," I said.

I let him pull me to my feet. Ease me forward. Inside his cool, dark, windowless office, Floyd switched on a lamp. I sat. The couch was soft. And Floyd sat beside me. My body tilted toward his like a book.

After thirty days Victor got out of the brig. We went parking on a dead-end road that very night. A dirt road somewhere between Holly Ridge and Verona. Close by, Venus flytraps grew in some bog. One of the only places on Earth these meat eaters grow. Their nectar lures hungry insects in. Then the leaf halves squeeze closed, traplike.

Victor put his arm around me. Said, "So what'd you do while I was locked up?"

"When you were locked up?" I shrugged. "Not much."

"Oh yeah?" Victor said. "Not much? Well, that's funny. Because I know these guys. I mean I know these guys, see. And they say you were screwing around." My hand closed around the door handle.

"I got connections. Man, I know things. I thought you knew that."

I tried to ease the handle down.

"Whoa, whoa," he said.

Like I was a horse.

"Hey, jus' kiddin'. Didn't choo know I was jus' kiddin'? C'mon, baby. Can't believe choo believed that," he said. He tightened his arm around me, vice grip.

"Nothing happened!" I said.

"'Course not," he said. "That'd make you a liar. And I hate liars. You know that. You know. You know what we do to liars in Paterson. Don't choo, baby? Huh? Yeah. You know. Buzzards, baby. Buzzards, same as worms." He laughed. A laugh like a whisper, a secret that's just been told. "But I'm jus' kiddin', baby. You know that. I know you wouldn't lie to me. Would choo? Would choo, baby?"

I was glad it was night. Glad it was dark and he couldn't see my blood had climbed to my face.

"I'm goin' away, baby," he said, unbuttoning me. "I mean, I'm goin' to the 'Nam. I can't believe it. Can you? What choo think of that, baby? What choo think of that?"

His blade. Pressing into my chest. It didn't hurt, much. It felt like a punishment I had to bear. I told myself, *It'll be all right*. But I was scared and whimpered and bawled anyway.

"Do you think I might die, baby?" he said. "Zat why you're cryin'? 'Cause I ain't. Victor ain't gonna die. I'll be back. Come back for what's mine. Yeah, baby. Yeah." He ran a hand over my chest. "That's good, baby. That's real nice. Now put on your clothes, baby. Put them on while I drive. And when you get home you can take them off again and admire the my work."

When I got home and looked in the mirror, I thought, *It's strange*.

I've come to find out, there are other cases. Things like this happen in other lives and times. Years later, I read in the *Scout* about a doctor carving his name into one of his patients. Like artists signing their work. And about the man that knocked his wife unconscious, tattooed his name in black ugly letters across her chin.

Looking in the mirror, I saw on my chest the letters, scabby and malformed. The initials, VD.

If there's a Limbo, Victor Darkangelo's there. Waiting for prayers to bail him out. Not long after he started his tour of duty, I saw his name in the *Scout*, on the list of those killed. I try not to meditate much on him. But he visits me sometimes, oh yes. And at such times, I remember what darkness really is.

THIRTEEN

The door of the Pentecostal church was always open. Every time I walked by, I heard people praying to Jesus and to God. Day and night. One night, when Daddy was in town and Mama was sleeping, I went to see if Jesus was really there. To see if He might be waiting for me in the dark.

Waterville Holiness was one wooden room. No electricity. No running water. Lantern-lit. The sanctuary felt like the hot belly of a ship. Once my eyes adjusted to the dimness I noticed how paint was crawling off the whitened timbers, like dead skin. How glossy posters of Jesus were taped to the walls. *What a good-looking man*, I thought, *in those purple robes. And fine Turkish sandals like they sold at K-Mart, now all the rage.*

That night a woman was praying hard to Jesus. She lay on the floor and screamed, "Oh Jesus, oh

God." She cried, huge wet sobs from the very lowest part of her chest. She was so loud, so full of sorrow and desiring, I thought she could've been crying for all the sad people. All the sad women in the world. Even Mama. Even me.

She was Lauri Shack. She'd divorced her husband because he wouldn't come to Jesus. Because she didn't want to be unevenly yoked. Making her sound like an ox.

"Don't you get lonely?" I blurted out once, weeks later, after we'd traveled to seaboard towns together in the bus a few times. Witnessing.

She said everything was all right. She was married to Jesus now.

The congregation of Waterville Holiness witnessed locally. But the seaboard towns, as I'd later found out, had become their true calling. It was the preacher Green Stokes's dream to start a new church in Morehead or Beaufort. For some reason he thought people in these towns really needed to be saved. Their disposition made them harder to witness to, he said. I asked him, "Why, Green Stokes?" He said individualism. Born of a love for the sea.

That first night I visited Waterville Holiness, I told the preacher Green Stokes I'd seen my boyfriend's name earlier today in the *Scout*. Listed among the dead.

"How old are you, girl?"

"Fifteen."

"Fifteen! Girl, I'm sorry for your loss. But do you think you have any business with a *boyfriend*? I do *not* think so."

"We prayed together in his car," I lied. "We counted beads. Read his Holy Cards."

He said those rituals are sinful. It was worshipping idols.

"I don't worship idols."

Green Stokes said, "Yes you do. You worship hair."

Green Stokes was a retired Marine with a wild past, it looked like. His arms were covered with tattoos of naked women. One of the women did a bump and grind whenever he flexed his arm. He could hide his tatoos, I'd later hear him tell his congregation. But what for? His tattoos were testament of his love for God! How far he'd come in his spiritual destiny!

He was balding. *Which might explain his obsession with hair*, I thought.

"Hair? I don't worship hair."

"The Virgin's hair. Locks of the Virgin's hair. In all the Italian churches."

"I don't go to Italian churches!"

"They also worship holy girdles," Green Stokes

said.

"Girdles?" I asked, thinking of those garments with panels, belts, and hooks that Mama used to wear.

"Not Sears and Roebuck," he said, apparently reading my mind. "Study your mythology. Learn what the other kind of girdle is."

I looked at him with what must have been surprise and alarm.

"And they worship a basin. The basin, girl, used at the Last Supper!" His lips and cheeks quivered. "Three shoulder blades! Five arms! Fifty index fingers! Thirteen heads! In these churches! Sister, you're in deep peril."

My heart pumped hard. He said, "You'll be all right."

"Preacher," I said. "Did you ever feel like you were bleeding? Draining blood, but from the inside?"

He tisk-tisked and shook his head. "God bless you," he said. " You must not give up," he told me. "You must not give up like that poor girl Lydia Hunnycutt just up the street. Self-murder's a sin, and you'll be punished for it." He put his chubby hand on my forehead and prayed some gibberish words. His hand felt like a warm raw steak. The muscle in his arm tightened and released, making the naked woman dance.

When he stopped praying, his eyes bored into mine. "Let's get serious," he said. "You'll be all right. But you must accept Jesus. These are the last days. You don't want to be left behind."

No. I didn't want to be left behind. I'd never wanted to be left behind. It was lonely that way.

"Listen!" Green Stokes said. "If a friend. No, that ain't right. If your *best* friend, came to your door what would you do?" His eyebrows were raised, pleading. "You'd let them in wouldn't you?"

Silence.

"What would you say to them? You'd say, 'Come in,' wouldn't you?"

No I wouldn't. I'd always understood Mama didn't like company. She never invited people into our home. But at the same time, I did know what Green Stokes meant. Normal people did that. They did it all the time. So I nodded. I said that, yes, I'd let them in.

Green Stokes seemed relieved. He reached, tore down a poster of Jesus. I saw Jesus was blond and wore a beaded necklace with a cross. Looked like He just got back from the beach. It made me wonder, *Where's the surfboard?*

"Take this," Green Stokes said. His chest heaving, expanding to indicate his generosity.

I liked the poster. Jesus wore a leather strap on

his wrist. It looked like a great big watch, the fashion now. I knew Jesus was supposed to be a carpenter, but He didn't look like one. He looked more like a hippie. Mellow like that and kind. All happy about the eyes. And His long, gentle hands weren't blistered, callused, and scarred. He wasn't missing any fingers. His hands weren't like any carpenter's hands I ever saw.

"Well, it's the same with Jesus," Green Stokes said. "If He knocks at your heart's door you've got to let Him in. You've just got to. You ain't got no choice. You've got to do it right now. Will you? Will you invite Him into your heart and life?" His tone got even more serious, then. "Because if you're not with Him, you're against Him, little girl."

I knelt with Green Stokes. Said, "Jesus, I accept you."

Men came from the shadows of the church and stood around me. They put their hands on my shoulders and on my head. Turned their faces heavenward and prayed. Cried out hard in the throes of some passion I couldn't understand or feel. I came to understand that when men prayed at Waterville Holiness, they did so in bunches, in flocks, like birds. While the women usually prayed by themselves. They'd go to a quiet corner of the church. It was like being in a closet with Bridegroom Jesus, they said.

"There's His sacrifice," said Green Stokes. "Something's owed. You've reaped. It's time to sow."

That very Saturday, I rode the bus with the Pentecostals. To seaboard towns. To spread the word of God.

FOURTEEN

I was sixteen when I noticed the blood. I saw the stain, shaped like a giant beetle, growing blurry and fat, spreading across the back of Mama's housedress. I noticed it when I was weeding the zinnias and she'd come outside to hang the clothes. That night her blood soaked her bed. And the next week the doctor told Mama and me how much the cancer had already spread. Far and wide. From stomach and loop-di-loop intestines to the far countries of lungs, heart, and brain. It grew in her uterus like a greedy child. Mama listened to the doctor silently. Each moment worsening. Organs disintegrating without sound.

They admitted her to a room, where the nurses bathed her and inserted IV tubes. I didn't mention the snow. The radioactive snow from the West. Instead, I gritted my teeth with love. Mama frowned at my life, the one she'd always been too afraid to criticize. She didn't condemn me now. She only asked over and over, "Will you be all right?"

"Yes, I'll be all right."

She said, "I didn't pay you enough attention."

I said, "It's fine, Mama. Mama, I'm sorry, but Daddy won't come."

She was quiet a while. Then she grinned. "I guess I won't get them ten years to do whatever I want. Didn't I tell you, Pearl? Didn't I tell you once he'd be here even when all the roaches are gone?"

Which was to say, misery lasts.

Then she told me how he once wrote lovely things. That in letters from the war he used to call her honey and sweetheart. That he used to think of her as part of his own body. Just as much as his own leg or arm. "But he's different now," she said. "He ain't the same. They all change like that. They all do." *Zeke wouldn't*, I thought. *Zeke wouldn't change like that.* All this happened on the first day.

On the second day, Mama held her belly. Pain ebbed and flowed. Her face went grim, then took on a look of agony. A wave licking the shore. Leaving something unpleasant behind. Then taking it back. Leaving and taking. Over and over again.

But she never cried out. She never made a sound. She amazed the nurses, who never realized how much practice she'd had.

Lauri Shack had a base decal on her car bumper, so there was no problem getting on Camp LaGrange. I don't know why she had a decal. Maybe her earthly husband had been a Marine. She drove me to the Naval Hospital to visit with Mama. Lauri Shack said she didn't mind. That Jesus expects you to do good works. She studied her bible while I visited. Or went to the hospital chapel to pray.

On the third day, Green Stokes came with us. Laid hands on Mama and prayed.

On the fourth day, Mama said, "Daughter, I messed the bed." And it was horrible for her. Her worst nightmare. This soiling of public sheets.

"Let me help you."

But she said no. "Not your job. Get the nurses. They're used to it, I reckon," she said. "Somewhere," she said, as she was being wiped, "in this same hospital, babes are being born. Aren't they? Aren't they, Daughter?"

"Yes, Mama. I suppose they are." I'd turned away. Trying to give her some respect. Some privacy at least.

"Yes, suppose they are." Her voice trailed away, thinking about the voyage ahead.

I thought about heads crowning between women's legs. Babies being pushed into the terrible light. No wonder they cry.

After Mama soiled the sheets, she stopped eating. During the next four days, when no one was looking, she'd even pull out her IV's.

Then, in the late afternoon, as I was riding to the hospital with Lauri Shack, maybe as Lauri Shack and I were driving past columns of sweet-faced boys marching on the fields, one of Mama's major organs failed.

So it is, I've thought many times. *How everything that opens, closes. Moss roses. Venus fly traps. Hands. A life.*

- - -

Lauri Shack wanted to go to the hospital chapel to pray for me. A man I recognized from Waterville Holiness was in the chapel when we arrived. He told us he'd come to pray for anyone in need, and the nurses had directed him here. Had said he couldn't go in strangers' rooms. He was Brother Harvey Moss. Old. Pencil lead thin. Spoke with a bad wheeze. Maybe ill himself. His eyes were imploring behind thick glasses as he told us the hospital wouldn't let him do God's work.

Lauri Shack offered her condolences as she and I sat on a bench.

"I guess I ought to love them, even as they block my way," the brother said.

"*Pray* for them," said Lauri Shack.

She put her hand on my back, raised her other arm, tilted her face heavenward. The old man touched my shoulder and prayed in tongues, that obscure language. I stayed, let them beseech, but told myself, *After this, no more of this touching.* I felt no comfort in it. Just a vast emptiness. Like the day-time sky was inside me. Limitless. Blank. *Just leave me*, I was thinking. *Leave me to this vacancy.* Only hands that could have saved me—Zeke's. No, I'd not forgotten that. When Zeke had ushered me in and out of all the stores. And his touch had made me feel safe. Later, I'd still go to church, but I didn't let anyone touch me. I'd go to a dark corner, lie on my back and pretend to pray.

At home, the trailer windows were all dark. I knew Daddy was home. That somebody had called him. A doctor or a nurse. To tell him she was gone. And there he was, sitting at the table, eating. "Hello, Daddy." He said nothing. What did I expect? Arms outstretched? Crying together? Reconciliations? I went into the bedroom to change my clothes because I felt soiled by others' hands. The trailer door slammed. The truck's. The engine growled and he was gone.

- - -

Waterville didn't have a crematorium. When I told Green Stokes my plan, he told me burning bodies was pagan. That you were supposed to follow Jesus in all things. And they'd buried Jesus. I was disappointed to hear this. I'd hoped he'd help me. "But I can't bury my Mama," I explained. "She wouldn't have wanted a public grave."

"Little girl," he said. "That just don't make sense. Your Mama's with God."

I wondered, *Why can't I burn her then?*

Next, I went to Floyd. And I was so grateful when he got right on the phone, using it like a magic instrument to make things simple. And this ease by which he did things, it had a big effect on me. I'm not exaggerating—that day I thought this man could part waters. Mama's death now bound us, almost as though by blood. Every boy or man I'd ever known had left me. But not Floyd. Now he'd helped me do the best I could do by my Mama's poor dead body. How can you thank a person for that? Yes, he helped me send her to New Bern, and drove me up there so I could get her and carry her home. "This is what she'd have wanted," I told him. Yes, Floyd helped me with everything. Paid, too.

"There, there," he told me. He said it was no trouble at all.

I buried her ashes in the sand underneath the trailer, the only place that ever felt completely safe. As I buried her, I thought about the Pentecostals.

About the day both Lauri Shack and Green Stokes had prayed for Mama. How Lauri Shack had fallen under the spirit and lain on the hospital floor. Prayed so well, I'd thought, *Maybe God will grant her prayers.* Wondered, *How could God say no to such persistence as this.* Lauri Shack was married to Jesus. Could Jesus really say no? Green Stokes had prayed earnestly, too. In the name of Jesus, with his meaty hand pressing Mama's head deep into the pillow. The tattoo of the naked woman had danced, but her head had been cut off by his sleeve. Green Stokes had the gift of healing, he always said. "Miracles happen," Green Stokes told his congregation often.

But I'd been noticing, regardless of prayers, people died all the time.

― ― ―

The same day I buried Mama's ashes, I tried to cook a meal for me and Daddy. I tried to make fried chicken like Mama had. I left the cooked chicken in a big bowl on the kitchen counter. I sat at the kitchen table a long time and waited for Daddy to come. He never came.

I went to bed and stayed two days, curled into a little ball.

I didn't get out of bed for anything. Not even to eat.

One day, the thought crossed my mind, *Ham-*

burger. And then I got up and walked to Buck's. It was simple as that. *Hamburger*.

Cleopatra worked there then. She came to my booth, wiping her hands on a thin striped towel. Said, "Pearl." Just the sound of my own name was enough to make me cry. Cleopatra took off her hairnet and the hair fell into her eyes. Just the way I'd always remembered it doing. "How's your Daddy?"

I hadn't seen Daddy since Mama died, but imagined he was at Saigon Sal's. I felt safe in answering, "Pretty much drunk all the time."

I looked to the moth-eaten buck for understanding. Here was something familiar, and I grasped onto that. The buck's eyes, glossy-black like two dead worlds, said everything they needed to say: *He already knew; nothing could change this*.

Cleopatra's smile was pinched back, frugal. But it was kind. She was truly sorry about my situation, I knew.

I saw black spots on her teeth. *My God*, I thought, *she's rotting right in front of me*. It made me want to tell her something. A secret we could share. Just the two of us. I could whisper. Low. Then, ever after, whenever Cleopatra and I saw each other we'd have this. This secret. It'd cement us. I could tell her that the night Mama died I cooked fried chicken.

Left it on the kitchen counter, like an offering. The sight of it, Cleopatra, I could say. *Untouched. The bony pieces, cold in the bowl. Carcass-like.*

Messy. Messy. Messy. Messy demands the body makes.

Or *My family's strange*, I could say. I could say it out loud. It'd be a relief. *A side-show kind of strange,* I could say. I could say, *Cleopatra, did you ever go to the Onslow County Fair and walk past the sideshows? Past the man asking the crowd, "How could they survive?" Past the hootchie-kootchie girls in their slippery clothes?*

I wanted to say these things to Cleopatra. But instead, I felt my pants pockets and blurted out, "I don't have any money." I hadn't thought about that until just that moment. But it was true. I was broke. Until then, I hadn't thought about where my money would come from. Mama had always scrounged what I'd needed from Daddy's wallet or from his chest of drawers. I hadn't even thought about how I'd stay in school.

Cleopatra brought me a hamburger, and a heaping plate of fries. So many fries that they spilled out onto the table like golden treasure when she set the plate down.

"This ain't no food shelter," a woman shouted from the back. Through a large opening in the wall, a kind of shelf where the cook placed finished orders,

I saw the woman who'd said that. She heaved raw patties into a blackened pan. She was old. Looked like she'd been at that stove a long time. Years.

"Yes ma'am, I know," Cleopatra said, taking her own purse from under the counter and paying for my food. "I'm paying."

The bell on the cash register rang, and so did Cleopatra's coins.

"This ain't no food shelter," the woman said again. Lower this time. Unhappy. Not quite satisfied. She flattened the sizzling patties with a spatula. Lifted her head, sniffing for some pleasure she'd somehow let by.

What could I say to show my appreciation? Something nice? Something meaningful? Something that would really help Cleopatra in her life? Something to let her know I'd seen the agony she'd been through?

There was so much to say. I loved Cleopatra, felt drawn to her, thankful. In a sense, she was saving me, saving my life. My spirits were on the upsurge because of her. And these facts weren't lost on me. But I was also torn. Because even knowing her turmoil with Floyd and how she'd sat crying in the wet grass, even knowing how Floyd's belt had broken and bruised her sister Lydia's skin, I'd have had to say to Cleopatra, "I love Floyd." I would've had to say to

Cleopatra, "I love Floyd." I would've had to tell her, "I love your own daddy." Worse, I loved him in more than one way. Not just as a daddy, I'm trying to say. I don't think she'd have liked hearing that.

"Cleopatra," I said, "I *will* pay you back."

She shrugged.

"I *will*, Cleopatra. I *will*."

"Neither here or there to me," she said before proceeding to refurbish the ketchup bottles at each booth, wiping the bottlenecks down before she rescrewed the caps. Wiping the bottles' mouths so clean.

I took a bite of the burger. Daughter, what can I tell you? Sometimes, there's consolation in grease. The way it soaks in and flavors the bread. The way it delivers salt to the tongue.

I never did pay her back. No, I never did.

- - -

After Mama died, Daddy spent all his days and nights at Saigon Sal's. Never came home again. Guess he spent his time telling people his wife was dead. And his daughter didn't understand him. I guess he showed his photograph of Steve McQueen to anybody that'd look. "I brought Steve McQueen through boot camp! Goddamn Steve McQueen!"

The state could've taken me, but Floyd said, "Come stay with us. And go to school. I'll take care of you."

FIFTEEN

Inland folks don't much fear hurricanes. Think, *I'm safe from the long arm of the storm.* Which was the problem last year with Hurricane Floyd. Everybody thought wind, not rain. Folks going to bed bracing for maybe a renegade wind awoke to black water filling their houses. People stood, helpless and small, on the islands of their roofs.

Whole families clung to cedars, waiting for deliverance. Or drowned and were caught in the arms of the trees. Until the waters were filled with bloated horses. Pigs. Goats. Dogs. Chickens.

Human bodies that had floated out of graves.

Hurricanes are conceived in the doldrums. Which, as in life, is a place marked by frequent squalls and periodic calm.

Hurricanes, many here believe, are the hot wet breath of God.

Floyd the man, now that's a tougher case.

I loved him.

And one night soon after I moved in with Nan and Floyd, just as it was bound to, it happened.

Had I acted in a tempting way? Tossed my hair back and blushed? Exaggerated the swing of hips and thighs? Yes. In fact that very day I'd dressed in a miniskirt and fishnet hose. Put a good slow song on the phonograph. Something bluesy. Danced a pleasing little dance with a slinky scarf. Nan too had danced at first, then bowed out to watch. She clapped for a while, encouraging me, then fell silent, invisible, like she used to when I won at cards. I thought of Green Stokes's tattoo. Danced like the woman danced on his arm. I was watching Floyd. I saw it in his eyes. He really liked me. When the song ended, the needle kept thumping on that empty space at the end of the LP. Yet Floyd seemed lost in time and didn't move. Neither did I. It was Nan who put the record away. Tucked it back safely into its jacket. Broke the spell.

And Floyd Hunnycutt, once the daddy of my dreams, did he take my warm and silly seductions in his hands? My hips in his hands? The curve of my neck in his hands? And in his mouth? Yes. Yes. And yes. I thought about his magazines. The broken girls. *Go ahead*, I thought, *Undo me like that. Spread me out like that. Crack me open like a nut or a lobster's claw. Let it happen. I'm sixteen. Make me look like that. It's what I want.* I'd settle for that. I thought I had to.

Let me start again.

I lived with Nan and Floyd. Ate with Nan underneath the tapestry of the Last Supper. Underneath Christ, so strong in His bones and busy with His dying. The giant fork and spoon hanging on either side.

We ate. Myself. Nan. Floyd. It was my job to scrape our plates clean. Nan washed. I rinsed. I was sixteen.

Sometimes, I went to seaboard towns with the Pentecostals.

Sometimes I lay down with Floyd. I don't know how many times. I don't remember. It's only the first time I remember. But, oh, there were other times.

Jesus would never want to marry me.

This is how I remember it. The first time. Waking to the sound of water roaring in the pipes. Floyd standing over me, a wet shadow, bathrobed and cologned, while I pretended to sleep in Cleopatra's bed.

My time, I was thinking. *My time. My time. My time.* No more planting little seeds of touching. Our fingers on that little red ticket that said, *Admit One.*

This is what I've wanted all along.

Don't be surprised. Look at my story. This moment was all prepared for. His lap. His flattery. The way he cheated so I won at cards. Our fingers touching on that little red ticket at the Orb. Each ingredient measured through the years. Look back. And don't hate me.

For so long, I loved words. Words, words, words. This time, there were no words. Still, could the whole world hear this? One person passing through another? Sharp teeth clicking against mine?

I was thinking, *This is what I want.*

Hungry person that I was.

I was thinking, *The girls in the magazines. What was it about them he liked? Them opening themselves to him? Voiceless, obedient? What?*

- - -

Soon after I'd laid down with Floyd, I started seeing Zeke in Waterville on the weekends. He'd stand for hours in the shadows surrounding Floyd's house. In his camouflage clothes. Watching and waiting. It made me feel guilty, like a very deceitful girl. For ever since those cookouts at the Bells', hadn't I dreamed of being Zeke's girl? Still, I knew it was Floyd he was watching, not me. The *Scout* printed a story about how Zeke was following Floyd around Waterville again, nudging Floyd's Cadillac sometimes with the Galaxie. About how Zeke went to Floyd's furniture store. Where Zeke straightened paintings. Sat on couches. Rocked in chairs. Laid himself out like a king-size martyr on the king-size beds. I heard Floyd call the police once. But I guess they told him they couldn't do anything about Zeke, unless he'd hurt Floyd. Because Floyd yelled into the phone, "What have I got to do? Wait 'til he kills me?"

- - -

One weekend, I was drawn to the Bells' again by the smell of honeysuckle, gasoline, and fire. A fragrance I'd not experienced in a long time. Not since Dee-Dee and Clyde had wrestled in their yard. Not since Dee-Dee had been knocked out by hitting her head on the concrete duck.

Pentecostals were at the Bells'. Two men, fatherly-looking in their white shirts and sweater vests. Experts in seismology, as all Pentecostals are, they'd been drawn to the Bells' by the shifting plates of Zeke's obsession, which they'd read about in the *Scout*:

BOYFRIEND OF DEAD GIRL STALKS BUSINESSMAN HUNNYCUTT—
Girl killed self over love.

Clyde's fire was licking the food, which was all

crispy and black. Lumps of coal. Punishments from Santa's heartless bag.

The Pentecostals sat. Their hands resting like white rafts on their black-suited knees. "Son," one of them said to Zeke, "can we take you now? To the sanctuary of the Lord?"

"I just wish you'd talk to us," Dee-Dee said. "Zeke! Talk to us. Tell us what's wrong."

No reaction, except to rub the stubble on the back of his head with his fingers.

"Ezekiel," one of the Pentecostals said, "wouldn't you like to come with us, son?"

Clyde said to Zeke, "Go with them or stay. I don't give a flying fuck what you do. But I'm telling you. We're tired of your shit." Clyde looked mischievously at the duck. The white duck that wavered in the sun. The white duck with neon orange feet and bill. The one Dee-Dee liked to talk to instead of her husband.

"Ain't that right, Clyde?" said Dee-Dee's husband. "Tired of his shit, ain't we? Right Clyde? *Yes, quack-quack!*" Laughing. His eyes shooting to Dee-Dee. To the duck. To Dee-Dee, to duck. Dee-Dee, duck. Dee-Dee. Duck. "*Quack-quack!* That's right. *Ha, ha, ha. Quack-quack!*"

Dee-Dee shut her eyes hard.

Zeke. Rubbing the back of his neck.

"Son?" said the brother.

Zeke ignored them. The Pentecostals from Waterville Holiness wanted to give Zeke a new life, but they were too late.

Zeke had already found a new life. It was obvious. As manifested by his camouflage clothes. By the way he blended in with growing things. Looked himself like a green-growing new thing.

His new life. It was manifested by the empty dogtags around his neck, nameless and smooth.

This much I understood.

He'd already started life all over again.

SIXTEEN

Like Claudius, I was lousy at prayer. So I tried good works instead. They fit me like thrift store tweeds.

I, never the salesman, blundered from door to door. Covering my ears when housewives shouted, "Nosy women! Go take care of your own houses!"

Sometimes people let us in. I'd sit quiet and idly by as my partner, Lauri Shack, made people cry. She always focused on the last days and how hell awaits. She'd raise her arms and speak in tongues: "See-key, ro-bum, dee-dee, i." Old people cried and old people prayed. Prayed like they were putting extra money in the bank.

She made young people cry, too. The rapture would happen soon, she told them. Jesus would take His bride. I could see so very plain. They didn't want the rapture to happen. Not now. Not so soon. Not before they'd had sex. Kids. Seen their first snow. Stuck out their tongues to catch the cold flakes. Not before they'd touched the world like that!

The young people cried and the young people prayed. But in their voices and in their hearts I heard, *not yet, not yet, not yet.*

Lub-dub, Lub-dub, Lub-dub.

Not yet, not yet, not yet.

Sometimes, I even skipped school to ride with the Pentecostals in their bus to seaboard towns. Kept going because all along, they'd been promising me this: that the body that's been broken, cut, speared, splayed, cracked open, and scarred could live again. That the body that was hungry or thirsty could be filled. That it could be brand new and clean.

‿ ‿ ‿

One day, I found a kind of salvation. At the first of our appointed houses, Lauri Shack knocked on the door.

From his narrow bed, an old man called through his fly-specked screen door. Saying, "Come in."

Lauri Shack put her hand on the handle. "Not you," he said, and bluntly, too.

"What do you mean," asked Lauri Shack, "not me?"

"I mean not *you.*"

"What do you mean? Why not me?"

"Because I know you. I know your talk. Your talk of punishments. Last days. Your old and jealous God. Nasty old God. Stay away. Stay away. Stay away from me."

"But I've got good news!" said Lauri Shack. "God loves you. Please let me come in." It was an order to let her open the door.

"I will not."

"You will not?"

"No," he said.

"What do you want, then? For us to go away?"

"I want the quiet one. Quiet one, come in."

Lauri Shack rattled the handle.

"Not you! I said, quiet one, you. Come in."

I did. I sat in his only chair.

"Can I also come in?" asked Lauri Shack. She shielded her eyes to see better through the screen.

"No."

All his living in one room of clean, blond wood. He had two broken hips and said he'd be dying soon. We talked about the weather, boats. Dead parents. Dead children.

Lauri Shack's face appeared at the screen only once more. Saying, "Hello!"

"Go away! Out of my doorway!" He flung out his arm. "Git!"

And the face did as it was told.

"Listen," he said, finally, reaching for a tin cup. He spit tobacco in it. He held the cup before me. "Look. Nothing but this," he said. The cup was stained from his hands. From his spit. It was full of years. "Understand? Nothing but this. And then the grave."

I thought I understood. And I wanted to believe. With the sea licking my skin and my hair with its rough mother-tongue, I wanted to believe. His voice was powerful.

No, not powerful enough to chase my angry God away.

But I knew this. I'd never ride the bus again.

That night, Nan didn't come home. A meeting, I figured. The French Club or the Honor Society. She forgot to tell me. Floyd and I had eaten canned stew. Manufactured metal taste. Sucking on pennies taste. Sucking on bullets taste. Floyd had been jumpy all evening. He was sitting in his recliner, looking at the TV, but the TV wasn't on. Then we heard the *Foomp-oomp-oomp* of Thrush mufflers.

Nan had told.

This much I know now. She was in a cinderblock cell. Sitting. Waiting. Waiting for the truth to let her out. She'd told that day at school. And school counselors and police had already called

Floyd on the phone, asking questions. Floyd knew the trouble he was in.

I know now. The police had talked to Zeke, too. Who'd said Lydia had told him many things. Would they like to hear? And hearing, would they believe?

It was only a matter of time, Zeke had told them.

"A matter of time?" they'd asked.

Oh, there'd been so many chances already. Chances to avenge. So many times it could've been done. He'd followed Floyd all over town on many days. To Floyd's places of work and his places of play. Places of play like *The Other Place*, an XXX bookstore with little Peeping Tom machines that played movies of naked girls for 25-cents. He'd seen Floyd at *The Other Place* so many times. Followed him in. Watched Floyd push his eye against the lens. "I had my knife," Zeke had told the police. "And thought to slit his throat. Right then. Right there. As he looked at naked girls. Oblivious."

Now Floyd's long white finger was to his mouth. *Shhhh.*

Floyd and I must have made such a picture. Me sitting close to him on a small table he kept by his chair. Me, a little object, an adornment.

And we heard the kitchen door open and the kitchen door shut. Softly. Politely. The way Zeke always treated doors.

I said to myself, *Everything's all right.* But I knew it wouldn't be. I *knew.*

Because I felt all the sharpness in the room. Nails behind the paneling, sharks' teeth pointing in. Electricity running needle-like through wires. The scratch-scratch of fiberglass insulation.

I felt splayed and speared. Thrust through. Dizzy. Turning, turning, turning on a spit. I felt Zeke's knife. It made the scars on my chest ache. Though I could see it was sheathed in his boot.

"Easy now," Floyd said. "Steady now."

"It's time," Zeke said. Looking down at a make-believe watch on his wrist.

It's time, it's time, it's time, I thought. In rhythm with my turning.

"Yes," said Floyd. Cool, vampire-easy.

"You know it's time." Tap-tapping on the make-believe watch.

Zeke came close, bent at the waist to look Floyd in the face.

Time will save his ass. Didn't somebody say that once?

But who was it needed to be saved?

Turning.

"Yes. Yes," said Floyd. His arm, a snake striking. Into the pocket of his jacket, out.

His mouth. Just time for a grin.

I was dizzy, but I saw. He pulled the trigger *himself.*

And his brains. They spattered our clothes. Our face. Our hair.

For months and months at Hollingsworth, as I faced window or hall, I tried to pick them off. Floyd's brains.

Jackie O. From where did you get your strength?

SEVENTEEN

My first year at Hollingsworth, drugs. I stayed curled into a ball for a year. Nurses rotated me, facing window or facing hall. Through the window, I saw leaves clapping in the trees. Limbs falling on graves. Watched the sky flame and darken. Over and over. Over and over again.

I was haunted by dreams of blood and God's searching eye.

Saw the dead drifting in and out. Mama making food, chomping bones and burnt bread. Lydia, glistening like a sleek fish, her bruises oiled and gleaming. Floyd, taking tickets behind glass. Red vampire mouth behind glass.

There's a graveyard at Hollingsworth where girls are planted. Like seeds. I used to think about them like that. As seeds. Dormant under the clipped and mulched grounds.

I felt their presence. Talked to them.

I want to die, want to die, want to die, too, I told the dead girls at Hollingsworth.

They sighed. *Good grief. Why? We don't want you. We're too busy with our own deaths.*

But, I said. *I'm tired and have bad dreams.*

Squabble with your dreams, then.

God stares at me. All His judgments. All His stipulations and demands.

Let God do what God does. Let Him. Live your life.

But I want to go back to the Earth. It's the natural way.

It's better to be above the ground and clean. To be dressed freshly, not in rags. To grind your teeth on mistakes instead of dust. Mistakes you might remedy at last. Who knows?

I'm tired and want peaceful sleep.

Back to this again? Then sleep! All us girls, lying together shoulder to shoulder in our wooden boats, we've told you how to deal with sleep before. There's no sleep here. Don't you understand? Don't you get it? Our sockets are always open!

Nurses came. Phantoms in rustling clothes. Turned me on my other side. Toward the hallway now. To watch the endless motion of legs and wheels.

There were days near the end. Days I did my

shorthand. A complex mechanism. I needed to see something kind. A woman like Ida Deal come with brownies for her boy.

There were days.

       ‑ ‑ ‑

I must have shown promise at Hollingsworth. Though I'll never know what they saw in me. But during the second year they taught me a skill. Mrs. Boney, a shorthand teacher from a local business school, dictated to a few of us every day. She always read the same two paragraphs from *20th Century Typewriting*:

> *A successful office worker is a complex mechanism, a combination of a lot of things. He is, primarily, one who possesses all the skills his job requires. He can work quickly and accurately. He is not lazy, nor does he waste time. He is proud of his work, and his superiors have confidence in him.*

And

> *Assuming he is not basically lazy, a man with the right job does not wait for five-o'clock, nor does he dread the arrival of Monday morning. Sooner or later he will realize that work is neces-*

*sary for us. If man did not have work occupying
his hours, he would have excess leisure and the
monotony that results from it.*

During that time, I wore snappy pantsuits. I had
skills. I worked quickly and quietly and accurately. I
was a complex mechanism. I stayed in line. It even
helped me to feel my fountain pen gliding so freely
across the green steno pad.

Then, near the end of that second year Daddy
drove his truck into a swamp. He was drunk, the
Scout said, and a rifle was across his knees. But the
newspaper revealed it wasn't a bullet, it was water
that took him. Though the water never rose above
his knees. Hypothermia, the *Scout* said. The para-
doxical response to sudden cold.

Coincidence for my parents to have died so
close together in time? Why so? Why so, when there
are so many ways to die? All kinds of ways to die.
Peril on top of peril. Ask the Kennedys. Read Shake-
speare. Look at the *Scout*.

I was just reading the other day about a little
boy visiting his mama's grave with his daddy, and
in a flash his daddy was dead. Why, his mama had
been dead just a week. The headlines in the *Scout*
were:

BOY SEES DAD HIT BY LIGHTNING, KILLED—
Freak of nature happens at grave of boy's mom.

I try to imagine that. Clouds darkening. Maybe a cool breeze darting through the hot air, flickering over the boy and his daddy like a tongue. Their spines, boy and man, ramrod cold, knowing. Then the strike.

Or maybe not. Maybe the sun was out, a beautiful day. Maybe there was only a little patch of darkness, a black drawer in the sky with something dangerous coiled inside.

The little boy, orphaned within a week. Who would've believed?

So many ways to die. Crashes. Water. Poison. Heat and cold. Body's slightest malfunction. Act of nature. Act of God. Murder. Suicide. War.

Tragedy begetting tragedy. Death begetting death.

When it rains, it pours. And so forth. And so on. Like that.

"I can't believe it," I said, when a therapist told me the news. For so long I'd believed Mama. That he'd outlive us all.

The therapist had been assigned to determine whether or not I could leave Hollingsworth. She was new and didn't know me at all, only what she'd read about me in my file. Don't ask me what she looked like. Hollingsworth was a revolving door. A brief stop for therapists on the way to higher paying jobs, I'd heard nurses say. Only enough time to stretch their legs! So you didn't pay much attention to how the therapists looked. You only endeavored to do like they said or like they wished. To act in the manner they saw fit. So I was at a loss when the new therapist handed me a copy of the *Scout*. Watched me read.

"Is this a test?" I wanted to ask. I was wondering if I was supposed to cry, or not. Throw a pencil or a shoe? Kick over a desk? Sit down and put my head in my hands? Laugh and say, "I'm glad he's gone"?

It was such a little article. So few words.

"Are you all right?" the therapist asked.

So few words to describe a life, a death.

My eyes shifted to another article. One about snow-suited anglers on Lake Erie. A place where, the *Scout* said, springtime means an avalanche of mud and robins. Ice on thaw. The lake's cold, white heart melting. Trapped on an ice floe, the men floated far, far, and far.

Imagine. Floating off from everything you know. What homesickness is that? For dirt. For fireside. The smell of food cooking. That warm steam that coats the insides of your nostrils. Even for the taste of grease. Hamburger. For familiar rooms. A blanket that once kept you warm.

The fishermen were rescued, the *Scout* said.

A chance to fish another day.

Tomorrow. I concentrated on that.

And then, out of sadness and joy both, I wept. I knew.

I was all right.

After Hollingsworth there were days I set aside for research at the public library, for going through back issues of the *Scout*. I had two years to catch up with.

I read that Nan was at a university in some Ohio town. A town with brick streets and houses with stained glass windows built during oil boom years. That's what the Waterville *Scout* said. Geraniums, the article said. Geraniums in window boxes, geraniums beside the heavy wooden doors. They'd done a special feature on Nan, in the *Where Are They Now?* section. It talked about how well she'd adjusted to life after her tragedy. This was the last I ever heard of Nan. But I've wondered.

Had she tried to act old because her father was drawn to little girls?

Did it hurt when she told?

If I could see Nan again I'd sit at her feet. I'd tell her: *I honor you.* I'd say to her: *Nan. You were brave.*

— — —

After I got out of Hollingsworth, I spent many hours in front of big, bulky machines. Looking up facts through the miracle of microfiche. What else I found out ... Before Zeke fell into the wells of Lydia's black love ... Before the bunny bus ... How to say this? Say it.

It was in the back section of the *Scout*. What I need to tell you was with all the oddball news. News of food thefts. Like the man who stole one beer from 7-11. One beer. Just one. Because he'd been working all day, laying tar on roads. And he was tired. And he was thirsty. And he had no money that day. No money at all. *No*, they told him. *No credit. You must pay.* He was very thirsty, he said, and he'd pay. Tomorrow. It'd have to be tomorrow. He got his check then. They said *no*. He took out a gun. Tomorrow, he promised. Tomorrow. And sat outside on the hot pavement next to the 7-11 to drink. And drink. And drink. He emptied and crushed the can. Sat heavy in his guilt until the police came and carried him away. This is worth stating—it wasn't a real gun. This thing I have to tell you was with the oddball news, like mazes cut through fields. By Aliens? Bizarre cruelties of every kind. You know how people are.

It's not clear exactly how the *Scout* knew this. But it was her daddy's. It was Floyd's.

The *Scout* said Cleopatra and Nan told that Floyd had been with all his girls. Telling each, "Hush and give me a little." Or, "Do it with me. I'll leave the others alone." Nan and Cleopatra told how each sister had offered themselves in their sisters' place.

I said it. I said it now. Before Lydia had sex on the bunny bus and then became Zeke's girl, she'd been eight weeks with Floyd's child. No clinics then. Abortions were against the law. So she'd been spread out on the Bonecutter brothers' table. Pressed down, smoothed out, flattened by morticians' hands. Scraped clean by tools in their hands. The *Scout* said Floyd was there. For the whole procedure. I try to imagine that. Him there when she was shaved, and swabbed, and emptied by the Bonecutter brothers. With metal tools. *He was there*.

"I'll kill them," Steve McQueen had said in *Love With The Proper Stranger*. "Kill them if they touch you!" That was always Mama's favorite part.

That's the way it was. Imagine that. Can you? Lydia, the one that dropped the meat patty on her sister's plate? Her body among cosmetics and fluids? Curved needles for sewing eyes and lips shut? Can you see it? Feel it? The Bonecutters' bright light? The cold metal table? The dull tools? No wonder

Zeke couldn't stop her distress.

The Bonecutter brothers never went to trial. They disappeared. To some other country, no doubt. They had money enough to put everlasting distance between themselves and the law. I think they knew not to end up in the same place as Zeke. If I'd been them, I would've been scared to be housed with Zeke Bell.

After I read about Lydia's ordeal in the *Scout*, I told myself, *This is darkness*. And tell myself now, whenever I see Victor or Floyd, whenever they rise from their graves and visit my home, *This is darkness*. Not the darkness of blurry edges that comforted me once. The darkness with edges that guided me through the world. No, this darkness sleeps in my bed and dirties the sheets. Tosses and turns like a grumpy lover. Washes its head in my kitchen sink. Won't flush the commode. Pets me. Strokes me from behind. Fingers my throat. Unbuttons me. Slow and slow. One button at a time. Puts a knife to my skin. I feel the sharpness of knees. This darkness illuminates me. The shadow I cast is a stranger to me. I stare. Naked. Wondering who I am.

Was this the same darkness Lydia had felt, the darkness that'd made her eyes so deep and black? The darkness that had drawn me in and made me so curious about her world? Was this the knowledge I thought I wanted?

I try to clean my home. Fumigate my thoughts. Scab, scar.

But never heal.

EIGHTEEN

What did Brian Lily know or think of me? That I was old enough to be his mama? That I wear odd hats? That I saw murder? Maybe even took part?

He must have thought about it. Told himself before he ever lay down with me in the sheets, *She was with that boy, Zeke Bell, and they killed that man. Two gunshot wounds to a man's head. Zeke went to jail for thirty years. Pearl went to Hollingsworth for two. She got out, learned a craft. But stayed a little crazy. Yes, definitely stayed a little crazy.*

The day after he'd come into my home and touched my loom, the very next day, he returned. As I thought he would.

He stood at my door, speechless. As pine cones loosened on the trees and fell—*whack! whack, whack!*—onto my roof. Perpetual scattering of seeds.

Brian Lily stood at my door like a poor boy with

his pants pockets turned out. Like a boy forfeited of all his words. I liked that, and I let him in.

I, survivor, stood at the beginning of a new millennium. A thousand years to do what I wanted.

What did I want to do?

The truth? I hadn't much ambition. No ambition, really. Other than to move and be moved. To be caressed. Like a ball before it's thrown.

No. No illusions of love. Just touch. That's all. The chance to feel myself existing. The way you can only exist between somebody else's hands.

NINETEEN

Victor Darkangelo once told me about two kinds of Limbo. One for sinners. And one for the sweet little babes that died before they could be baptized— theirs, a natural state of bliss.

I used to think maybe there was also another kind. A place our spirits lived before we got trapped in the flesh.

That night, after I'd been to the back side of the Orb with Bruce Baggott, after I'd spat in the dirt, after I'd leaned against Floyd like a book, I sat on a bench and watched people skate.

It was the first time I'd ever thought about what aloneness really means.

At midnight, as the lights went down for the last time, couples orbited the floor and kissed in the shadows.

But I wasn't watching lovers.

I watched one lone boy.

He formed a circle with his arms, a circle like the world, the long, bony fingers of each hand just touching, and wove in and out of couples on his black skates. I watched until he was the only one I saw. Nobody else. Just the boy. Then I quickly shut my eyes.

And the image of him stayed. This boy. He made loneliness into something a person could want.

Into a kind of wisdom the world needs.

PART III

ONE

I meet them now at my door this morning, saying, "Go take care of your own houses. I don't like the company of others."

Which sounds like a lie, of course, considering the condition I'm in.

And, in the dumb way of cows, the Pentecostals stand their ground. Fishers of men.

"You aren't leaving," I observe.

"No," the old one says. "We came back. Like we told you yesterday." She pauses. "God has sent us."

Let's get this over with at last.

"Very well, but I prefer to hear God's message outside."

I choose a straw hat with a wide brim to keep out the sun. A souvenir hat from Topsail Beach with pipecleaner gulls that have crazy, googly eyes. With seashells glued to the leather band. The silliest hat

I've got.

We sit in the back yard on rusty metal chairs that are sad-looking, like the skeletons of once-great ships.

Spook is underneath the trailer, panting. She gives us all the look of scorn we deserve. It looks cool there. I wonder how the Pentecostals would feel, crawling under the trailer and lying down. Talking about God in the presence of Spook, Mama's ashes, some spiders, and the occasional snake?

They're talking about the mystery of God. But my mind's on more earthly things. Like the cruelty of people.

"You're here to find out who she belongs to," I say.

"*She?*" asks the old Pentecostal.

"My daughter."

"Daughter?"

"I know she's a girl," I say, "because I felt her soul."

Devil's in this woman for sure, the old one's thinking. Even so, she's glad to get it all into the open. "You may tell us who it belongs to. If you wish," the old one says.

"Did you love him?" the young one asks. "The father of your baby? The father of your little girl?"

"Baby," the old one corrects.

"Baby," says the young one, blushing.

I turn to the young one. "You want to know about *love*," I say. Sigh heavily. "Understandable. Once I was curious myself. But men are dark things, like windows boarded up to shut out the light. Like shadows. Like dark mists across the waters."

The old one's testy. She interrupts. "God is love," she says. It's like a big dark period stamped at the end of my sentences.

"Like dark mists across the waters," I say. Putting the period there myself. "Maybe it's true, as you say. But many's the time I've prayed, asking about love. I never got an answer."

The old one says, with disgust she can't hide, "Maybe you loved the wrong things."

Sinners are bad, but a backslider. Oh, Daughter, that's worst of all. For once you've experienced the sweet hand of God, they think, how can you turn back? It's the worst kind of treachery.

I say, "I want to tell you something." She thinks I'm ready to *divulge*. Which of course is what she's come for.

"Just a little secret." She's ready to hear it.

I tell her, "We sometimes all love the wrong things."

TWO

Mrs. Phoebe Marshburn arrives just as I get into it with the Pentecostals. I say, "I've got business to do."

The old one says it's all right. They'll wait.

Phoebe sits in her air-conditioned car with her old dog Pudgy, a terrier she dresses in doggy hats and tees. He's on top of a stack of sheets in the back seat, stiff as a corpse. Wearing a bucket hat and a T-shirt that says Surf City, the location of Phoebe's store. He raises his head to look at me. Beneath his hat, I see the glazed-over, bloodshot eyes of a living thing begging for release. Phoebe never goes anywhere without Pudgy. She's afraid he'll die. He's old and has old age diseases. It's only her presence, her voice, her touch, some connection they have, she thinks, that keeps him alive.

Phoebe, like most people of means in Waterville, drives a Cadillac. Hers is black as a hearse and always stuffed with merchandise and other matters of her essence. Today she's brought rags. Her floorboards and seats are covered with them. Her trunk, I know, is full, too. She pushes a button and lets the window go down. The window goes up-down-up until it's the way she likes, open just a crack. "Well, howdy!" she says. Her voice is thick with money, Southern grace and charm. And just plain good business sense. She powers the window down a bit more, enough to extend her cool fingers for me to touch. I do. It looks like a gesture of royals. She waggles my index finger and then her hand retreats. The window slides up a little. "Well, Ah've brought you some raw materials Ah'm sure you've got use fowah!"

I size it up. Good load, for the most part. Lots of thick cottons, flannels and corduroys. Good colors. Both brights and earth tones. But there are a few thin sheets and factory ends that look like cotton-poly blend. Seeing them annoys me momentarily. I don't like fake cloth, and Phoebe knows this. It's slick and crawls out of the weave even after you've beat it back with the reed. It doesn't make a good tight rug at all. It's the material of last resort. None of this matters to Phoebe. To her, cloth is cloth. Business is business. More cloth is more business. More business is better business. And so she's brought all the cloth she could find. In truth, I'm thankful. And I tell her so.

The trunk pops open. There are eight paper grocery sacks of old clothes. I get my wheelbarrow, nestle in the bags, and roll them to my steps. I carry the sacks into my trailer two by two.

Glancing out the window, I see the old Pentecostal sits rigid in her chair. Bible in her lap. Looking straight ahead. The young one rests her chin on her hands, her elbows stabbing at her legs. They're here for the long haul.

When I go outside again, there's Phoebe, standing next to the car with her old dog in her arms. Pudgy's hat has worked its way down to his neck. The car's still running, still spewing its cool air. Phoebe and the old dog are wilted. Tragic-looking. Ancient Mary, dead Jesus. Phoebe talks to the dog. She tries to be peppy. *I wuv you Pudgy-wudgy, love you, love, mooah, mooah, mooah,* a fake kiss, *you sweet Pudgy-wudgy, you sweet Pudgy-dog, Mama's sweet baby boy, yayuh, mooah!* Pudgy moans and lifts his half-blind eyes to hers. His eyes speak magnitudes: *Good Lord, just let me go.*

Of course Phoebe loves the dog. And so she sees things differently. Who can blame her for that?

I load the wheelbarrow, emptying the back seat except for two of the thin poly blend sheets for

Phoebe to lay Pudgy on. She puts him in the car on the sheets.

Now it's time. The real business. My money, the new supply of rugs.

"Ah hope you've got me a good load," says Phoebe. "Ah declare Ah'm all sold out!" Phoebe hands me the check.

I can work quickly and accurately.

I'm not saying I like it. Just that it's the way things are. Lemonade from lemons, as they say. With recurrence enough to gnaw off the ears.

Phoebe stands at the base of my steps. She never comes inside my home. No one enters, she understands. And she respects this. She only wants the rugs, which I bring her by the armfuls. She wheels them in the barrow and loads them in her car.

I possess all the skills my job requires.

I don't ask her about Brian Lily. I know I'll never see the boy again.

I am proud of my work, and my superior has confidence in me.

THREE

"I don't want to tell you who the father is," I say. "Would you believe me if I told you I don't care who he is myself?"

Which isn't entirely true. Because I think about him. A good deal. After he'd shared my bed, I didn't smooth the sheets for days. I stared and stared at his body's outline. *A man was there*, I thought. *Somebody warm. Who knew something about the body's gates. I think he was kind.*

"But," the young Pentecostal says, "a woman will always want to know such things."

"Why?" I say. "When like everything else underneath this dress—skin, hair, and tit—she's mine?"

"Does he know you're with child?" the old one asks, leaning a bit forward. "It could be he means to do right by you."

He doesn't know.

"Let me think."

"Think?" says the old one.

"Yes. It looks like you must have the name of my baby's father. It looks like you won't leave until I've given you one! So, I must think for a moment about how this must be told."

The young one's glad, giddy like a fawn, looks like she might frolic over the lawn. She thinks she's about to get the information everybody wants. But the old one's keen to get on with it. "Yes," she says. "Think how it must be told."

The ground is wet and smells of worms. The Pentecostals shift on the hard chairs, waiting.

"Well, I've thought about it. And I've arrived at a possibility."

"A possibility?" says the old one.

"Yes, a possibility."

"We're ready to hear it."

"Well, now. Think where we're sitting. Right here on the coast, not so far from a place called Ocracoke. Home of Blackbeard's ghost."

"Yes, this is true," says the old one. "Not so far away."

The two Pentecostals try to make sense of this. I can see their brains doing a sort of mental crochet.

"Do you know how he got his name, Blackbeard? His real name is Teach, you know. Edward Teach."

"Teach?" says the old one.

I almost feel like I'm instructing the old one how to talk.

"Yes, Teach."

"No," the old one admits.

"They call him Blackbeard because he used to braid his beard. Really," I say, "you have to think of the simplest things first."

The old one grunts. "Yes, and so?"

"He made many a woman walk the plank, I've read. Women taken as concubines for ransom. He sent them on to the silence of the fish."

The young one winces.

"I wouldn't worry," I say. "Some people actually like fish. Respect them even. For instance, the Carp ..."

"Well, yes, get on. So. Who's the father then?" says the old one.

"It's true, isn't it?"

"What?" says the old one. Impatient. Yelling the word.

"That so many roads must stop when they reach the sea?"

Blink-blink goes the young one.

"What in the world are you getting at?" says the old one.

"Okay, so what I'm getting at, what I'm trying to

say is, maybe it was *him*."

"*Him?*" says the old one.

Both of them, blink-blink.

"Yes. Him. Blackbeard, I mean, who came to me in the night and left me with a little girl. A girl he'd stolen from the ages!"

"Nonsense!" the old one explodes.

"Why? Why can't it be Blackbeard? Why *not* his ghost? To me, all men have been similar phantoms."

"I won't listen to this nonsense!" Fire slips out at the corners of the old one's mouth as she quotes scriptures. Her words twist around her like tired, old snakes.

"Blackbeard!" I clap my hands. Singing the name.

"I can see you won't let us help you," the old one says. "Foolish woman. But we're going to pray for you anyway."

"I'd always want to know who the father was," says the young one, crushed.

They pray. Bending their heads to the grass. I watch them. How their prayers hang loosely around their ankles. Like pious underwear.

⸜ ⸝

After the Pentecostals leave, I go to my pantry and consider everything.

Befitting a hermit, I eat simply now. Food in its

purest form whenever I can. An apple. An egg. A loaf of yeasty bread. But my pantry is also filled with food I've preserved, to get me through rain-soaked weeks and the occasional cold winter day. A hamburger at Buck's when I feel in need of grease.

Standing here in this pent-up place filled with canned jellies, meat—pigs' feet and tongue—I know there's no feast without death. And storing against the loss is a painfully slow way to die. And that there are quicker ways. I've considered them all.

Drowning. It might be peaceful down there, drifting along, the fish nibbling away.

Or hanging. There's a pine in back with a strong enough branch. By the time they found us, my face would be blue. Like arctic ice. And the note pinned to my dress would be delightfully confusing: *Bury us beneath the roses, please. Let them suck our bones. Wrap their tendrils around our hearts. The shifting and settling of the earth will sing us a lullaby.*

Yes, I've thought about it. But I've decided, no.

Somewhere, there must be somebody whose heart flickers. A warm fire in all this bitter foolishness. And that person would feel something. Wouldn't they? A spasm just behind the rib cage? A coldness in the bowels? I don't want to make anybody feel like that.

Another reason. *Not* because I'm afraid of God.

Or hell. Because people will decide I killed myself because the Pentecostals finally taught me shame.

FOUR

I get down to the work of making a new batch of rugs. Here's Mama. As usual, inspecting all the nooks and crannies. All the secret places. Asking, *How much of this is what you plan to leave behind?*

Lydia complains, "This isn't how I planned my life."

"I know," I say. "It's all right, Lydia. It's all right. I love you. I really do."

Somewhere, in some cell, Zeke waits.

Somewhere, in a place where evidence is kept from many trials—saliva, semen, hair, all the telltale leavings of human acts—his prints are on a gun. Two bullets from this gun are in a sterile bag.

Two bullets. *Two.* Do you see what I'm saying? That Zeke's in prison for shooting a dead man?

But who'd believe that. Would you believe my story? Coming, as it'd be, from a pregnant hermit woman, former resident of Hollingsworth who talks to dead people. Who wears odd hats. And has the letters VD carved on her chest?

Outside, Spook chases her things that go thumping in the dark grass. My trailer goes *Ping!* A pipe gurgles.

One time I watched *Leaving Las Vegas* at the Iwo Jima, a once magnificent theater but now a much forsaken place. Well past its former glory. I've always watched movies there, not at a ticky-tacky mall cinema. I've always gone to the old Iwo Jima with the heavy door, the cracked reptile-like seats. With its great length of wooden floor. Its chipped plaster. Its gurgling pipes that sound like they're alive. Like the sounds mothers make when they digest their food. When you come out of a good movie at the Iwo Jima, you're reborn for a while.

I was taken in by the main character, the man more in love with death than he was with life. And by the angel midwife that guided him delicately through that changing of worlds.

A man in front of me, watching the movie alone, like me, laughed from time to time at Nicholas Cage's jokes. The man was lonely. And his laughter came to me through the darkness like a question mark about his own survival.

This must be what the Indians felt, I thought.

When almost all their people were dead and on the other side. When they'd been driven out of their homes. Loneliness like that. Homesickness like that. What Jackie felt. And Ethel. Caroline. What Bobby felt when he made this note to himself: The innocent suffer—how can that be possible and God be just. *It must be what the wolf feels that gnaws off its own leg to escape the bright jaws of the trap it's in. The fly. Trapped between the sweet hinged leaves of a plant named for the goddess of love.*

- - -

I'm sewing now, stitching these rag strips tongue to tongue. Waiting for you to come like a brand new millennium. Like a brand new hope. Like Bobby's little ripple of hope.

How people prepared for the crossing to a new millennium. Batteries. Water. Generators. Food. And when the hand swept past the twelve and nothing happened, when the electricity still surged through wires and water through pipes, when no planes fell from the sky and no foreign powers humbled us with bombs, when Jesus didn't come and take us away for His bride, many must've felt flat. A dread. How could they face it now, that sameness?

But it's this sameness that I love. For instance, this cutting, this sewing, this beating back the reed, this stomping on the treadle. Over and over. Every day.

Oh I do have plans, pretty patterns I'd like to someday try. Still, in this sameness I make something skillfully with my hands. This is the meaning of craft.

Skill and love. Coming together. In this sameness, there's always a chance. A chance for another day. I have tomorrow.

If there's a God, couldn't He be in this sameness, this doing? This doing that's a kind of starting over? Like a baby pulling the world to itself again and again? This renewal, this healing?

Couldn't God be in this, and not somewhere else? Not waiting like an angry lifeguard with a whistle in His mouth? Not waiting with all the keys to punishment's doors jangling in His great big hand?

Couldn't He be?

Because today, while sewing and weaving, while waiting for you, I've had this longing to lie down where Hurricane Floyd happened. In places where even now people's wounds are fresh. And to say to them something I think's akin to wise:

You floated past dead pigs and horses, past cedar trees where little drowned children came to rest. You climbed the stairs to attics and roofs as the rivers filled your homes and covered the heads of gods in your churches. And though you've got your regrets, hands reached for that drifted away, you were saved, and that's your center now. You hung on to your scant lives.

Now when you see the sun, take it. And when you see the rain, remember. The rain's still a blessing when you consider how much water in a lifetime a person drinks.

Look at the sky. Think, even as you fear its bigness or its darkness or its noise, one day you might forgive it.

A little. Be thankful. Yes, be thankful! And, above all, be earnestly kind.

I've got plans is what I'm saying. That's all I'm really trying to say. I survived. And I've got plans. I'll tell you a secret. I'll whisper. And when I do look at you at last, we'll have this. It will cement us. This is the truth. I am a complex mechanism. I have dreams at night. In which Zeke reaches between my thighs. Peels me.

It's like I'm a hot and delicious fruit. One just discovered. One not yet known by humankind.

I still dream about Zeke's hands. And how they find me. At last. In the dreams I rise to his hand as to the surface of water. I gasp. My lungs fill with air.

ACKNOWLEDGMENTS

I must first thank Anika Streitfeld, my editor at MacAdam/Cage. Her care and expertise were invaluable to me as I worked through the final drafts of this novel.

I must also thank the editors of the following literary journals for publishing excerpts from *The Secret of Hurricanes* in a slightly different form: *The Chattahoochee Review*, *Sulphur River Literary Review*, *Seems*, and *Visions International*. Thanks especially to James Michael Robbins, editor of *Sulphur River*, for the letters of support he wrote to me as I was attempting to find a home for my book. Without the affirmation these journals provided, this novel would have never been completed.

There are several inspiring teachers I would also like to acknowledge: Ralph Croom, my tenth grade English teacher who died too soon; Bill Hallberg,

Erwin Hester, and Douglas McMillan, my English professors at East Carolina University, precious jewels all three; and Philip F. O'Connor, my creative writing advisor at Bowling Green State University, who nurtured my will to write and taught me to persevere. I would be amiss if I didn't also thank George Core, editor of *The Sewanee Review*, for commenting on several of my stories through the years.

Finally, thank you, Daddy, for teaching me to say my ABCs and to count at four. Thank you, Mama, for believing I could one day write a book. I'm so sorry, both of you, that you didn't get the chance to see this happen.